SHERLOCK

C000064806

MYSTERY MAGAZINE

#11 (VOLUME 5 NUMBER 1)   January/February 2014

THE ONE WOMAN SHERLOCK HOLMES FEARS:
MRS. HUDSON

" I WANT NO MORE DEAD BODIES ON THE
CARPET, NO MORE BULLET HOLES IN THE WALLS,
NO MORE VIOLIN PLAYING AFTER TEN O'CLOCK
AT NIGHT, NO PIPE SMOKING, AND NO MORE
COCAINE, OR OUT YOU GO. "

MARC
BILGREY

Publisher: John Betancourt
Editor: Marvin Kaye
Assistant Editors: Steve Coupe, Sam Cooper

Sherlock Holmes Mystery Magazine is published by Wildside Press, LLC. Single copies: $10.00 + $3.00 postage. U.S. subscriptions: $59.95 (postage paid) for the next 6 issues in the U.S.A., from: Wildside Press LLC, Subscription Dept. 9710 Traville Gateway Dr., #234; Rockville MD 20850. International subscriptions: see our web site at www.wildsidemagazines.com. Available as an ebook through all major ebook etailers, or our web site, www.wildsidemagazines.com.

FROM WATSON'S SCRAPBOOK

Once more Holmes and I must do without the offices of Mrs Hudson for some time to come, inasmuch as she is nursing her ailing Aunt Ruth in Yorkshire. Her daily rounds and our personal needs are being ministered to by our landlady's friend Mrs Warren, and whereas her cooking is not as interesting as Mrs H, it is perfectly adequate. Of course, we cannot include in this eleventh issue of *Sherolock Holmes Mystery Magazine* the usual column that Mrs Hudson normally contributes, but Mrs Warren has agreed to try her hand at a bit of authorship.

Otherwise, I am pleased to offer no fewer than three Holmesian tales, the business of a countess who went missing, the Paradol Chamber adventure that I earlier alluded to (in each instance I made my own notes available to Messrs Grochot and Koons so they could do their best to understand my lamentable handwriting and chronicle those cases); also included is my retelling of the somewhat risible case of the Red-headed League.

I pointed out to Holmes that I also prevailed upon Mr Dan Andriacco, of Ohio, to write an article pertaining to a well-known American detective and his chronicler's agent, Mr Rex Stout, but I could not elicit any comment at all from my friend and room-mate other than to say that for "legal reasons" his lips are sealed upon this subject.

Now for a few words from my colleague Mr Kaye.

—John H Watson, M D

Now that SHMM is on a bimonthly publication schedule, I am pleased to report that fictional submissions have kept pace with the demand for more content—both Holmesian and non-Canonical ratiocinative adventurings. But alas, our nonfiction folder is not in as healthy a condition, and we are therefore much in need of new contributions. If you think you have something to interest us, please describe the article you would like to write for us in a message sent to me at marvinnkaye@yahoo.com (and do note there are two n's in the middle of the address).

In this the eleventh number of Sherlock Holmes Mystery Magazine, several non-Watsonian exploits include a clever ghost story solved by a Jewish cantor (mind you, not the rabbi!) as well as a new Marc Bilgrey piece and the latest of Kelly Locke's semi-Holmesian cases by Hal Charles. Both of the latter authors also will appear in our next issue, as will regular contributors Gary Lovisi and Jack Grochot, and Fran Valentine is booked for a return engagement.

—Canonically Yours,
Marvin Kaye

COMING NEXT TIME...

STORIES! ARTICLES!
SHERLOCK HOLMES & DR. WATSON!

Sherlock Holmes Mystery Magazine #12
is just a few months away...watch for it!

SCREEN OF THE CRIME

by Lenny Picker

The Devil's Feet: The Cornish Horror On TV and Radio

For many admirers of the Canon—whether diehard Sherlockians or just casual fans—the most memorable passage in the sixty stories is Watson's description of witnessing the terror of *The Hound of the Baskervilles* first-hand ("A hound it was, an enormous coal-black hound, but not such a hound as mortal eyes have ever seen.") But for evocation of horror, there's another, less-well-known passage that gives Stapleton's demon dog a run for its money—after all, Watson was expecting to see some type of canine at the time:

> "I had hardly settled in my chair before I was conscious of a thick, musky odour, subtle and nauseous. At the very first whiff of it my brain and my imagination were beyond all control. A thick, black cloud swirled before my eyes, and my mind told me that in this cloud, unseen as yet, but about to spring out upon my appalled senses, lurked all that was vaguely horrible, all that was monstrous and inconceivably wicked in the universe. Vague shapes swirled and swam amid the dark cloud-bank, each a menace and a warning of something coming, the

advent of some unspeakable dweller upon the threshold, whose very shadow would blast my soul. A freezing horror took possession of me. I felt that my hair was rising, that my eyes were protruding, that my mouth was opened, and my tongue like leather. The turmoil within my brain was such that something must surely snap. I tried to scream and was vaguely aware of some hoarse croak which was my own voice, but distant and detached from myself. At the same moment, in some effort of escape, I broke through that cloud of despair and had a glimpse of Holmes'ss face, white, rigid, and drawn with horror—the very look which I had seen upon the features of the dead."

This section, with its air of Lovecraftian menace (published six years before HPL's first story, "The Alchemist,") is, of course, from "The Adventure of the Devil's Foot," which Doyle himself ranked as his ninth favorite short story. As with Hound, its power stems from the introduction of a supernatural element into the hyper-rational world of the Master. And the murderer must surely rank as one of the most sadistic in the Canon. The plot framework is familiar and easily summarized, although a bare bones description does not remotely do justice to the story.

SPOILER ALERT—*If you haven't read the story, please stop and do so before proceeding—you will regret it otherwise, as an analysis of treatments of it require discussion of the solution.*

It's 1897, and Holmes has given in to concerns about his "iron constitution," leading to a rare vacation with Watson in Cornwall. The setting affords Watson a prime opportunity to display his descriptive chops:

It was a singular spot, and one peculiarly well suited to the grim humour of my patient. From the windows of our little whitewashed house, which stood high upon a grassy headland, we looked down upon the whole sinister semicircle of Mounts Bay, that old death trap of sailing vessels, with its fringe of black cliffs and surge-swept reefs on which innumerable seamen have met their end. With a northerly breeze it lies placid and sheltered, inviting the storm-tossed craft to tack into it for rest and protection.

In that remote part of the world, Holmes's researches into the Chaldean roots of the Cornish language are interrupted, and his vacation becomes a busman's holiday. Tragedy has struck the Tregennis family, leaving Brenda dead, and her brothers Owen and George raving mad. The sole unscathed family member, their sibling Mortimer, had left them affably playing cards, with the only portent of what was to come a brief glimpse by George of an unknown something moving in the bushes outside the dining room window. And soon, the killer strikes again, leaving Mortimer also amongst the dead, on his face the same look of fear that marked his sister, and leading the local vicar to believe his parish is "devil-ridden." Displaying his typical brilliance, despite the strains to his system, Holmes deduces that Mortimer used the powder of rax pedis diaboli, devil's foot root, an obscure African plant, burnt in the fireplace, to remove Owen, George and Brenda from the scene. Holmes, less brilliantly, had tried the powder out, with almost fatal consequences for him and his Boswell. When Brenda's love, Dr. Leon Sterndale, who brought the devil's foot back with him from his travels, realizes what has happened, he achieves his own form of justice, one that, under the circumstances, Holmes and Watson endorse.

One of the many benefits of being a Sherlockian in 2014 is the easy availability of audio and video adaptations of the Canon that were lost to earlier generations. As a teenager in the 1970s, I found references, in books like Michael Pointer's *The Public Life of Sherlock Holmes*, to Arthur Wontner and the Rathbone/Bruce radio series almost as tantalizing as the good doctor's notorious untold tales. But today, much is accessible, and a recent viewing of the BBC's first Sherlock Holmes series, starring Douglas Wilmer and Nigel Stock, on DVD, prompted an assessment of how different writers have adapted the Tregennis case.

Eille Norwood played Holmes 47 times on screen in a series of silent films from Stoll Pictures; the second, from 1921 (as part of a series titled *The Adventures of Sherlock Holmes*) was "The Devil's Foot" (hereafter, just Devil). You can find the half-hour adaptation by Googling it; given Norwood's mark on the role in the era before the talkies, it's worth the time. The story is, naturally enough, compressed. The first title card sets the stage, with Watson reminding his companion, "Don't forget, Holmes, you're down here for a rest. Thank goodness there won't be any work for you here!" The pair then discover the Tregennises themselves—here all three, not just Brenda, are dead, perhaps because conveying the brothers's condition from the original—"singing snatches of songs and gibbering like two great apes"—was too hard to pull off in a silent film. There are some other minor changes—it is Holmes, not Watson, who pulls his friend to safety from the idiotic experiment Holmes undertakes to test the poison powder first-hand, but the general contours are included, even the clue of the gravel. The most jarring aspect, for me, was the inappropriate soundtrack, with jaunty music even at scenes of tension, and no segments where the instruments enhanced, rather than detracted from, the tension and suspense. And it's an uphill battle almost a century later to find a silent drama engaging.

1931 saw the first radio adaptation, starring Richard Gordon and Leigh Lovell, one that I have not yet been able to trace. But the second-oldest, from 1936, with Louis Hector and Harry West as Holmes and Watson, was easily locatable online. It's hard to tell if audio degradations over time have taken their toll, but the voices are an obstacle to engagement. Hector, in particular, sounds more like W.C. Fields to my ear than John Gielgud. This version opens traditionally, with Watson setting the stage—Holmes's break-down—before providing a word picture of the gloomy setting for their retreat from London. Perhaps guilding the lily a bit, the radio play's writer has Holmes point out that the treacherous bay called Mounts Bay in the Canon is known by the locals as "the Devil's Cauldron," and that the region was rumored to have been a center for satanic worship. The "strange monuments of stone" from the original are turned into remnants of a temple to the Dark One, who fled into the bay after its destruction, and whose "hoof-beats" could still be heard on moonless nights. The additions can't help put me in mind of the cinematic legend that a version of The Taming of Shrew was credited to Shakespeare with "additional dialogue by Sam Taylor." Doyle's more subtle descriptions are far more effective. Another problem is the climactic experiment scene, with Watson, instead of being possessed by a "freezing horror," narrating what he sees as if a play-by-play announcer, in what would seem to be an inevitable challenge for any audio adaptation. The adapter also has Sterndale identify the killer of his love to Holmes, who reacts, surprisingly, with surprise—when you eliminate one of two viable suspects, whomever remains, however probable, must be the guilty party. (See below for why Holmes should have regarded Sterndale as a suspect in all three Tregennis deaths).

Next to tackle the Tregennis case was *the* Sherlock Holmes for generations.

Basil Rathbone, in a radio play costarring Nigel Bruce as the lovable if unCanonical bumbler of a Watson. Sadly, I was not able to track down a recording, but surely Rathbone's iconic Holmes voice, with its air of superiority, made it a memorable one; and the other scripts for the long-running series adapted from the Canonical 60 took relatively few liberties. After Rathbone tired of the role, Bruce partnered with Tom Conway on the radio, and in 1947, the pair tackled Devil.

Conway does an excellent Rathbone, and by extension, an excellent Holmes. The script has some elements in common with the Hector version, e.g., the Devil's Cauldron, not too surprising with Edith Meiser at work on both series, and lifts whole sections intact from the 1936 version. Its Sterndale is only a neighbor of the Tregennis family, not a relative. Just two years later, Devil was again on the air, with John Stanley and Alfred Shirley in the leads. Like Conway, Stanley's rendition of the Master owed a lot to Rathbone's. The episode used a standard series device—presenting as prologue a climactic scene—here Holmes and Watson racing up some stairs in response to maniacal laughter by a man chanting "The Devil's Foot! The Devil's Foot!" After the sponsor's message, the listener actually hears all the Tregennis family in life, playing cards, and the scene includes Mortimer's reported observation of a lurking thing; hearing this first-hand makes more of an impact—the victims are characters the listener has encountered, and there's no reason at that stage—pre-horror—to be skeptical of Mortimer's account. That choice illustrates the range of options a creative adaptor has to enhance a Holmes story for the ear; for example, Bert Coules brilliantly opened his "The Adventure of the Dancing Men" with the murder already having occurred.

Unsurprisingly, Sherlockian Michael Hardwick's 1962 radio play was the most faithful to date, in keeping with the overall approach of the series featuring Carleton Hobbs and Norman Shelley. Unlike the other radio productions mentioned above, Watson's chilling depiction of the ill-conceived experiment was conveyed directly, with Shelley more than capable of evoking the terror his character felt at the horrific effects of the drug on his mind. And this productions's Mortimer actually comes across as a sympathetic victim at the outset, which better sets up the eventual reveal of his villainy. Hardwick's choice in making minimal changes to the text is validated by the finished product.

1965 saw the first video adaptation in over four decades, as part of the BBC shows featuring Douglas Wilmer and Nigel Stock. It's a pretty straightforward version, and one of the best in a sometimes too low-key series. It opens with the disconcerting images of the stricken Tregennis brothers and their dead sister, with wide-eyed Owen and George looking into the camera, gibbering out of their wits. This choice, in contrast with the Jeremy Brett version discussed below, plunges the viewer straight into the story, before introducing Holmes and Watson. The writer—Giles Cooper—takes advantage of every reasonable opportunity to supplement the story. Holmes checks what was visible in the bushes from the outside as well as from within. He's given a pawky quip to deliver at Watson's expense when the latter suggests the person in their cottage was just the housekeeper, Mrs. Pascoe—"not unless she's taken up smoking cigars." Watson has some valuable investigative work to do—interviewing the vicar to confirm Sterndale's statement that he'd wired him about the disaster, and after encountering Mortimer as well, he's able to help the case by sharing his impressions with Holmes, who clearly values them. It's Watson who experiments with a lamp to provide the baseline for determining when the one in Mortimer's sitting-room must have been lit. The viewer sees how exactly Holmes deduces that Mortimer dressed in haste on his last morning—a wrongly-buttoned waistcoat. The experiment scene is creepy with a bulging-eyed, crazy-looking Wilmer conveying the dramatic effects of the drug on his system.

Disappointingly, Cooper decided to tamper with one of the best-known exchanges in the whole Canon, as Holmes speaks to Sterndale in the final scene:

> "You then went to the vicarage, waited outside it for some time, and finally returned to your cottage."

> "How do you know that?"

"I followed you."

"I saw no one."

"That is what you may expect to see when I follow you."

The punchline, encapsulating the endearing arrogance of the character, is changed here, with Wilmer stating, "Quite understandable" in response to Sterndale's bafflement. Viewers may not share that characterization as the prolonged scenes of Holmes shadowing the explorer are short on actual stealth by the sleuth.

The richness of the source material made the 1988 telefilm for the Granada series one of Jeremy Brett's best outings. The opening is a bit of a spoiler—someone is seen breaking into a house, locating a vial as African drums play on the soundtrack, and pouring some of its contents into a container, leaving little mystery for a newcomer as to the cause of the Tregennis's sufferings. It's not clear why writer Gary Hopkins made that choice, which reminds me of the 1983 Hound, where a scene of Laura Lyons being strangled midway through removes any doubt that the scourge of the Baskervilles is an ordinary man. Edward Hardwicke's capable Watson pegs Mortimer a liar early on for claiming to have a blood disorder, which further vitiates the whodunit aspect of the story. Hopkins is more subtle elsewhere in tipping his hand; he shows Mortimer's version of events, with his brother looking past him out the window into the bushes, but rather than show Mortimer's false report of seeing something moving, he simply shows Mortimer narrating that part.

This is perhaps the most-familiar version for today's Sherlockians, and it's memorable for three things. Holmes's time alone recuperating is linked to his drug use, and the cocaine addict buries a syringe in the sand to signify his having kicked the dangerous habit—this is done well in advance of the experiment, and is not, as would have been contrived, a reaction to it. The experiment sequences features a nightmarish vision for Holmes, complete with images of Eric Porter's Moriarty, and a bleeding Holmes. But it's Holmes's recovery from the toxic smoke that caused the most comment—coming to his senses, Brett's Holmes yells out, "John!" This was apparently an ad lib by Brett, who noted:

"Well, Holmes is semiconscious at the time, right? It really was the one time that he could call him John. I think in extremis he might have said 'John.' It gives another slant to it. I slipped in 'John' just to show that, underneath it all, there was just something more than what they say, that Holmes is all mind and no heart."

Damien Thomas's Mortimer is a bit too shifty-eyed from the outset, but Freda Downie's Mrs. Porter—the Tregennis's housekeeper, whose recollections of the fateful night—and the horror of her discovery the next morning—are presented, and especially Denis Quilley's Sterndale are outstanding. (Gary Hopkins's recollections of his experience writing the script can be viewed online in a video entitled The Case of the Youngest Pen.)

As always, the BBC radio Holmes, with the ever-brilliant Clive Merrison and Michael Williams, enables me to end on a high note. Bert Coules opens with a depiction of the stress Holmes was under before his forced break in Cornwall—wrapping up a three-month case against an unnamed gang, and collapsing as a result of combining malnutrition with illness and a resort to the needle. Mortimer, the vicar and Sterndale are all introduced well before the first poisoning. The horror is conveyed with the sound of laughter, increasing in volume before degenerating into wild, despairing shrieks. Holmes's nightmare features the baying of the Hound of the Baskervilles, and manic laughter. The guest cast is solid, with Patrick Allen (Granada's Colonel Moran) as Sterndale, and Coules adds a joke Holmes makes at Sterndale's expense (when Watson wonders at his presence in England, Holmes speculates that, "perhaps he's finally succeeded in killing all the lions on the continent."). All in all, it is a perfect translation of the story to the form, and likely to remain as the gold standard for the foreseeable future.

Now, back to Sterndale himself as a viable suspect; a cynical reader of the story would note that he alone of the Tregennis clan ("upon my Cornish mother's side I could call them cousins," he tells Holmes) survives the action intact, and no other heir to the estate is identified in the text. Brenda is not around to confirm his account of their relationship, and Sterndale was much better placed than Mortimer to know of the effects of the Devil's Foot root, and to use it. Perhaps some future adapter will choose to add this theory to the plot, even if just for Holmes to consider and discount it, as he reasonably would have.

✗

Lenny Picker, who is always seen when he follows anyone (not that that is a regular occurrence), writes regularly for Publishers Weekly, and can be reached at lpicker613@gmail.com.

ASK MRS WARREN

by Mrs Amalie Warren

I do confess to a touch of nerves as I atempt to fill in for my dear friend Martha Hudson, who is off in Yorkshire with her convalescent aunt. Housekeeping here in the B apartment of 221 Baker Street is never onerous, except for the daily test of the digestions of Mr Holmes and Dr Watson. I have endeavoured to vary their fare, and so far I have heard no complaints, but that may well be an example of their gentlemanliness.

The doctor showed me a stack of correspondence addressed to Mrs Hudson, and has encouraged me to reply to some of these letters. I have selected three.

✗　✗　✗　✗

My Dear Mrs Hudson,

When, oh when, are you coming home again? I have been keeping busy helping Mr Holmes in a variety of problems which me and my "Irregular" cronies have helped with, but it just ain't the same to knock at the door and not see your beaming smile—not that I don't suspect you might wish I'd washed up better (at all!) before my arrival. Yet that has never stopped you from offering me a plate of biscuits and milk!

Billy

P S: The good doctor, with my hearty approval, has "cleaned up" my writing.

✗　✗　✗　✗

Dear Billy,

I regret that Mrs Hudson is still unavailable, but if you'll come tomorrow after the hour of noon, I promise you a plate of biscuits and a glass of milk (with a tot of gin in the latter).

Sincerely,

Mrs Amalie Warren

(filling in for Mrs H)

✗ ✗ ✗ ✗

My Dear Mrs Hudson,

I regret to report that every time I see a dramatic reenactment of one of Mr Holmes's detectival doings, the only Scotland Yard inspector who is ever represented is Lestrade, who, though a fine professional, simply was not always "on hand." Quite a few of these recountings really involved me, not Lestrade.

I do hope that you will set the record straight in an upcoming edition of your periodical publication.

Sincerely,

Inspector (retired) Tobias Gregson

✗ ✗ ✗ ✗

Dear Inspector Gregson,

Oh, dear! You have every right to feel disenfranchised! Dr Watson sends both his personal regards and regrets! Mrs Hudson is not available this month, but I shall see to it that your letter is indeed published in what Mr Kaye calls SHMM # 11!

With my sympathies!

Mrs Amalie Warren

✗ ✗ ✗ ✗

Dear Mrs Hudson,

I am a diligent devoteé of Dr Watson's stories, but in none of them is there any mention of the man whose surname you bear. I presume that he is deceased, in which case I do tender my condolences. I do hope it is no intrusion to inquire about him: his name, occupation, and whatever personal details may be fit to be revealed?

Curious in Cheshire

✗ ✗ ✗ ✗

Dear Curious in Cheshire,

Though Mrs Hudson is, at present, out of town and therefore cannot reply to your understandable interest in this little mystery, I am an old friend of hers (now filling in for her at Baker Street) and can afford some of the particulars for which you ask.

Archibald G. Hudson—better known as "just plain Archie"— was himself a private sleuth of no little reputation, though he could not compare with Mr Holmes, but then, of course, who could? His one ungentlemanly act was to leave his bride Martha here in London while he followed an investigation to New York City. There all record of him vanishes, though I have heard rumours that he took up residency somewhere on West 35th Street in Manhattan.

Mrs Amalie Warren

✗   ✗   ✗   ✗

I have done a bit of browsing in my friend Martha's preceding columns in this magazine, and note that on several occasions, she has set down the ingredients and procedural steps toward making food-stuffs that both Mr Holmes and Dr Watson praised her for. In this wise, I shall do the same and present two of my own dietary concoctions.

✗   ✗   ✗   ✗

LAMB CURRY

Do note, first, that this is not a dish from India, but rather, because of the presence of so much ginger, derives instead from Mongolia; second, this is indeed a spicy dish that demands an ample supply of beer or ale to wash it down—though if beef is substituted for the lamb, it will be a wee bit less fiery.

INGREDIENTS

1 lb lean lamb
1 tblsp set butter
1 onion
2 cloves garlic
3 tomatoes
1 large green, red or yellow bell pepper
2 teaspoons salt
1 teaspoon turmeric
1 teaspoon curry powder
¼ oz ginger
½ teaspoon chili powder
1 1/2 cups hot water—though beer or ale is a better choice

PROCEDURE

1. Slice, wash, defat meat
2. Fry minced onion, bell pepper, garlic, ginger, pepper in butter
3. Add turmeric, curry powder, salt and chili
4. Sizzle up to 3 minutes
5. Add meat and mix for a few minutes
6. Cover with lid and cook 35 minutes
7. Add sliced tomatoes
8. Fry for 2 or 3 minutes
9. Add liquid and bring to boil
10. Low flame for approximately 35 minutes, or till tender
11. Serve over flavoured rice (use wine, not water to make the rice)

✗   ✗   ✗   ✗

DEVILED LIMA BEANS

(One may also use butter beans)

INGREDIENTS

A small quantity of lima beans
1 teaspoon of very spicy mustard
6 ozs beer or ale
Seasoned pepper mixture (combine black, red, and white ground pepper)

PROCEDURE

1. Place ingredients in a saucepan
2. Add mustard and beer
3. Stir till mustard is well blended (but do not break beans)
4. Simmer slowly till liquid is reduced by approximately ½
5. Season with pepper mixture to taste
6. Serve in soup bowls with spoons

Very Truly Yours,
Mrs Amalie Warren

✗

THE ADVENTURES OF SHERLOCK HOOSIER

How Rex Stout Had Fun with Sherlock Holmes

by Dan Andriacco

The announcement last year that the actress Lucy Liu would be playing the part of Dr. Watson in the new CBS program "Elementary" attracted a great deal of interest—and also shock, skepticism, cynicism, derision, and scorn. In other words, the gimmick worked.

But a well known Sherlockian of the last century would not even have lifted one eyebrow at the news that "Watson was a woman." For Rex Stout knew that decades ago. On the evening of January 31, 1941, at the Murray Hill Hotel in New York, Stout declined to toast "the Second Mrs. Watson." In the talk that followed, he set forth for the assembled Baker Street Irregulars a scandalous theory that "the Watson person" who wrote the Canon was actually Mrs. Sherlock Holmes. Frederic Dannay, writing as Ellery Queen in the book *In the Queen's Parlor*, called Stout's speech an H-Bomb—H for Holmes, of course.

Stout cited many passages from the Sacred Writings that sounded to him as if they were written by a woman, and especially a wife, such as "I believe that I am one of the most long-suffering of mortals" and "I must have fainted" and "the relations between us in those days were peculiar." The *coup de grace*, however, was an acrostic spelling out IRENE WATSON from the first letters of canonical tales. Stout insisted at the end of his speech that the wedding related in "A Scandal in Bohemia" was actually Holmes's own, and speculated that the fruit of the union might have been Lord Peter Wimsey.

"As Rex reached his last sentence," John McAleer reported in *Rex Stout: A Biography*, "pandemonium ensued." He added: "In certain quarters 1941 would be remembered as the year that began with the Stout hypothesis and ended with Pearl Harbor—two nightmarish happenings."

Although Stout spoke from notes, a written version quickly found its way into print. So did an official BSI rebuttal from Dr. Julian Wolff called "That Was No Lady."

> Upon entering into a literary controversy with Mr. Stout [Wolff wrote], one is immediately conscious of being at a great disadvantage. It would require the knowledge and the pen of an Edgar Smith, the experience and the skill of a Vincent Starrett, as well as the genius and the beard of a Christopher Morley, to equalize the contest.

Wolff proved equal to the task, however. His response included an acrostic of his own that spelled out NUTS TO REX STOUT.

Long an admirer of Stout's Nero Wolfe and Archie Goodwin mysteries, I wrote Stout a letter when I was but 14 years old, asking him which story he considered his best and positing the bold theory that Archie was the true author of "Watson Was a Woman."

Stout fired back an ingenious response dated December 8, 1966. The postage on the note was five cents, but to me the contents have always been priceless. "Dear Master Dan," Stout wrote, "If your surmise, that Archie Goodwin wrote that gem, 'Watson Was a Woman,' is correct, I would be silly to admit it, and I try not to be silly. So the answer to your question, what do I consider my best story, is 'Watson Was a Woman.' Sincerely, Rex Stout."

Clearly, Stout liked to have fun with Sherlock Holmes. But he did so as a true believer who was one of the original Baker Street Irregulars and the Guest of Honor at that infamous 1941 meeting.

Born in 1886 in Noblesville, Indiana, Stout began reading Holmes as a boy and devoured the later stories as they were published. In 1903, having moved to Kansas at a young age, he saw William Gillette portray Sherlock Holmes in Kansas City. He returned again the next night.

More than a generation later, in 1931, Stout found himself among a select group of men drinking bootleg bourbon with Winston Churchill at a hotel in New York until the wee hours of the morning. One of the subjects of their conversation was Sherlock

Holmes. Stout was forty-five years old, and Arthur Conan Doyle had died only the year before—just three years after the publication of his final Sherlock Holmes story.

When Christopher Morley founded the Baker Street Irregulars in 1934, he asked Stout to be one of the first members. That same year also saw the publication of *Fer-de-Lance*, the first of Stout's more than 60 Nero Wolfe stories. More about that rotund gentleman later!

Stout's relationship with the BSI was a long and happy one. In 1949, despite the "Watson Was a Woman" blasphemy, he was presented with his Irregular Shilling and the investiture name of "The Boscombe Valley Mystery." For the first five years of the BSI's Silver Blaze Stakes at Belmont Race Track, Stout and his wife Pola attended, and presented the trophy in two of those years. In 1961, he was awarded the BSI's first Two-Shilling Award "for extraordinary devotion to the cause beyond the call of duty." Five years later, the annual BSI dinner again honored Stout and also toasted Pola as "*The* Woman."

Although best known as a mystery writer, the tart-tongued Stout was also a perceptive critic who was never shy about sharing his thoughts on his craft—or any other subject, for that matter. In January 1942, appearing with Jacques Barzun and Elmer Davis on Mark Van Doran's CBS radio show "Invitation to Learning," he made this observation: "The modern detective story puts off its best tricks till the last, but Doyle always put his best tricks first and that's why they're still the best ones." Later in the same program, he said, "It is impossible for any Sherlock Holmes story not to have at least one marvelous scene." (Obviously, he wasn't including pastiches.)

A few years later, in 1949, Stout wrote an article called "Grim Fairy Tales" for *Saturday Review*, in which he tried to explain why "Sherlock Holmes is the most widely known fictional character in all the literature of the world." And this was his conclusion:

"Sherlock Holmes is the embodiment of man's greatest pride and his greatest weakness: his reason…He is human aspiration. He is what our ancestors had in mind when in wistful bragging they tacked the *sapiens* onto the *homo*."

Stout added to this a more general statement which McAleer suggested could apply to Nero Wolfe and to Rex Stout himself. He wrote:

> We enjoy reading about people who love and hate and covet—about gluttons and martyrs, misers and sadists, whores and saints, brave men and cowards. But also, demonstrably, we enjoy reading about a man who gloriously acts and decides, with no exception and no compunction, not as his emotions brutally command, but as his reason instructs.

In an introduction to *The Later Adventures of Sherlock Holmes*, published in 1952, Stout argued that the success of the Canon depended on what he called "the grand and glorious portrait" of Holmes, which transcended the author's plot errors. "We are not supposed to reach real intimacy with him," he wrote. "We are not supposed to touch him." I have not yet had the pleasure of reading this introduction, but I gather from McAleer's description that it discusses Conan Doyle's literary offenses in some detail. And yet Stout concluded that all of these transgressions seemed to enhance the portrait of the Great Detective. How did that work? "No one will ever penetrate it to the essence and disclose it naked to the eye," Stout concluded. "For the essence is magic, and magic is arcane."

Stout wrote eloquently about Holmes again in 1963 for the cover of a record album of Basil Rathbone reading Holmes stories.

"Holmes," Stout wrote, "is a man, not a puppet. As a man he has many vulnerable spots, like us; he is vain, prejudiced, intolerant; he is a drug addict; he even plays the violin for diversion—one of the most deplorable outrages of self-indulgence."

But, Stout went on, there is much more to him than that: "He loves truth and justice more than he loves money or comfort or safety or pleasure, or any man or woman. Such a man has never lived, so Sherlock Holmes will never die."

Neither—I submit—will Rex Stout's most famous creation, Nero Wolfe. And since the fat sleuth's 1934 debut, readers and critics have drawn parallels between the two detectives. More than that, they have put them on the same family tree by speculating that Wolfe is the son of Sherlock or, less frequently, Mycroft Holmes.

Certainly Wolfe looks like Mycroft. And in the novel *Baker Street Irregular*, Stout says that the character was based on Mycroft.

In October 1954, as they appeared together at a book signing at Kann's Department Store in Washington, D.C., Frederic Dannay asked Stout how he came up with the name of Nero Wolfe. According to Dannay, Stout thought for a while and then said that he based the name on Sherlock Holmes. In McAleer's version, Stout was just quoting Alexander Woollcott's theory. Here's how Dannay lays it out in the book *In the Queen's Parlor*:

> Now…how in the world does Nero Wolfe resemble Sherlock Holmes? Well, one likeness is quickly apparent: both names have the same number and the same distribution of syllables: Sherlock has two, Holmes one; Nero likewise has two, Wolfe one. But this is a superficial kinship: the relationship is far more subtle. Consider the vowels, and their placement, in the name Sherlock Holmes. Sherlock has two—e and o, in that order; Holmes also has two—the same two, but in reverse order—o-e. Now consider the vowels in Nero Wolfe: Nero has two—the same two as in Sherlock, and in exactly the same order! Wolfe also has two—the same two as in Holmes, and again in the same reverse order!

Dannay called this "the great O-E theory," and mused that it probably all went back to P-O-E. Clearly, Rex Stout was not the only one having fun with Sherlock Holmes.

William S. Baring-Gould, in his biography *Nero Wolfe of Baker Street*, mentions the great O-E theory in passing in a chapter called "Alias Nero Wolfe," in which he argues that Wolfe is the son of Sherlock Holmes and Irene Adler. Frankly, in my opinion, Baring-Gould's attempt to prove a genetic connection between the two detectives rather limps. For example, in listing similarities between the two men, Baring-Gould writes: "In his youth, Nero Wolfe, like Sherlock Holmes, was an athlete." This is proof?

Undeterred by what seems to me very flimsy evidence, mystery writer John T. Lescroart adopted this paternity theory wholeheartedly in his books *Son of Holmes* (1986) and *Rasputin's Revenge* (1987). They recount the World War I adventures of John Hamish Adler Holmes under the primary alias of Auguste Lupa.

Lescroart's hero also calls himself Julius Adler and Cesar Mycroft. We are to assume that he later adopted the first name of another Roman emperor and anglicized the lupine last name. I personally found these books entertaining, but the series had short legs; it stopped at two.

As the Holmes-Wolfe connection kept being proposed over the years, Stout came up with a number of amusing ways of saying, in effect, "leave me out of this." As early as 1935, in a letter to the editor of *The Baker Street Journal*, he pleaded client confidentiality in his role as Archie Goodwin's literary agent. In 1968, he wrote to Bruce Kennedy, "Since the suggestion that Nero Wolfe is the son of Sherlock Holmes was merely someone's loose conjecture, I think it is proper and permissible for me to ignore it." A couple of years later he wrote to another admirer, "As for the notion that he [Wolfe] was sired by Sherlock Holmes, I don't believe Archie Goodwin has ever mentioned it."

And yet Archie Goodwin notes in *Fer-de-Lance* that he, Archie, has a picture of Sherlock Holmes over his desk. On August 12, 1969, McAleer asked Stout: *"Did Archie hang up the picture of Sherlock Holmes that is found over his desk, or did Wolfe put it there?"* Stout's response was typically unequivocal: "I was a damn fool to do it. Obviously it's always an artistic fault in any fiction to mention any other character in fiction. It should never be done."

We shall charitably assume that the reference to fictional characters reflects Stout's advanced age at the time.

Another interesting picture in the Wolfe establishment on West 35th Street is the painting of a waterfall, behind which Archie and others often hide in a secret alcove to observe and hear the goings-on in Wolfe's office. According to John McAleer, Stout surmised that the painting represented the Reichenbach Falls.

If Stout guessed correctly, this is quite appropriate—for Nero Wolfe and Sherlock Holmes both battled a criminal genius to the death. Professor Moriarty, a figure as archetypical in popular mythology as Holmes himself, is a significant presence in "The Final Problem," "The Adventure of the Empty House," and *The Valley of Fear*. He is also mentioned in three other stories. Arnold Zeck, Moriarty's counterpart in the world of Nero Wolfe, has speaking parts in the novels *And Be a Villain* and *The Second Confession* and appears in the third book of the trilogy, *In the Best Families*.

"I'll tell you this," Wolfe says to Archie in the first of these books. "If ever, in the course of my business, I find that I am committed against him and must destroy him, I shall leave this house, find a place where I can work—and sleep and eat if there is time for it—and stay there until I have finished. I don't want to do that, and therefore I hope I will never have to."

Like Holmes, he is ready to give his all. *In the Best Families* finds him doing exactly that. It's a kind of "Final Problem" and "Empty House" in one epic novel—epic not in size, but in terms of its significance to the Wolfe corpus. Wolfe isn't believed dead in the book, but he might as well be. He leaves the brownstone on West 35th Street with the door wide open and a strong indication that he will never be back. When he does return, months later, Archie doesn't recognize him. Physically he's a mere shadow of his former one-seventh of a ton, his face full of seams from the weight loss. His resolve and mental resources are undiminished, however. And by the last page, Zeck is as dead as Moriarty.

Julian Symons, an English crime writer and often-difficult critic, was effusive in his praise of what Stout achieved in the Zeck Trilogy, which was later collected in an omnibus volume called *Triple Zeck*. He wrote:

> In the fight to death between master-detective and master-criminal the most ingenious and unlikely subterfuges are used…All this is very improbable. It is the art of Mr. Stout to make it seem plausible…Holmes was a fully realized character. There is only a handful of his successors to whom that compliment can be paid. One of them, certainly, is Nero Wolfe.

Surprisingly, Stout told McAleer more than once that this story arc wasn't planned—that he didn't know for sure when he wrote *And Be a Villain* that Zeck would reappear in another book. That would mean, then, that he wasn't intentionally paying homage to Reichenbach and *The Return*. But who can doubt that Stout was influenced by the death and resurrection of Sherlock Holmes, however subconsciously?

Nor is this by any means the only impact the Canon had on Rex Stout and Nero Wolfe.

In Rex's appreciation of Doyle's art [wrote John McAleer], we find valuable guidelines for understanding Rex's own art. He saw the necessity of making Wolfe a man rich in human contradictions. Wolfe's eccentricities surpass those of Holmes. At times he is childish in his moods. He shuts his eyes more often than Holmes does to "moral issues." More than once he "arranges" for the suicide of a culprit, to save himself a court appearance. Yet, withal, even as Holmes is, he is "grand and glorious."

He also has a sidekick without whom he would be just another genius sleuth. The parallels between John H. Watson, M.D., and Archie Goodwin may not be immediately obvious, but they are strong. Like Watson, Archie is:

• his boss's Boswell (although better known in crime writing as a "Watson");
• a man of action;
• a ladies' man;
• the one who always carries the gun (although Holmes occasionally does, too);
• a colorful and interesting character, unlike S.S. Van Dine or the unnamed "I" of Poe's Dupin stories;
• a conductor of light, if not himself luminous.

In this matter, Stout's debt to Conan Doyle was conscious and acknowledged. In *The Mystery Writer's Handbook*, a 1956 volume from The Mystery Writers of America, Stout wrote an article called "What to do About a Watson." He argued that a Watson helps solve what he called "your main technical difficulty" of having the detective hero learn information that the author isn't ready to share with the reader. "A Watson can be a devil of a nuisance at times," he wrote, "but he is worth it for his wonderful cooperation in clearing the toughest hurdle on the course."

At the end of his three-page essay, Stout cited an example of a Watson at work for the author in this exchange from "The Red-Headed League":

"Evidently," said I, "Mr. Wilson's assistant counts for a good deal in this mystery of the Red-headed League. I am sure that you inquired your way merely in order that you might see him."

"Not him."

"What then?"

"The knees of his trousers."

"And what did you see?"

"What I expected to see."

"Why did you beat the pavement?"

"My dear doctor, this is a time for observation, not for talk."

And then Stout added—gleefully, in my imagination—"That's the way to do it!"

Nobody who has ever read Rex Stout's mysteries could deny that he did it his own unique way. But he was also operating under the spell of Arthur Conan Doyle's arcane magic.

The great private eye novelist Ross Macdonald expressed the opinion of many critics when he wrote:

> Rex Stout is one of the half-dozen major figures in the development of the American detective novel. With great wit and cunning, he devised a form which combined the traditional virtues of Sherlock Holmes and the English school with the fast-moving vernacular narrative of Dashiell Hammett.

Stout deserves full credit for doing this so well, and over a 41-year period. But Conan Doyle was there before him. While the first part of *The Valley of Fear* is an exemplar of "Sherlock Holmes and the English school," the flashback half—the story of tough guy Birdy Edwards in Vermissa Valley, U.S.A.—is arguably (as Steve Doyle writes in *Sherlock Holmes for Dummies*) "the world's first hard-boiled detective story."

So even in his best known and most enduring contribution to the American detective story, Rex Stout walked in the footprints of a giant. And they were *not* the footprints of a gigantic hound!

✗

TO WALK A CROOKED MILE

by Hal Charles

I

Kelly Locke had just gotten off the phone with her—what should she call him, she wondered—her significant other, when the doorman at the entrance of the Baker Street complex buzzed to let her know her father was on the way up to her second-floor condo. Originally, as Paul's baseball team had a rare day off, they planned that after she finished doing *The Six O'Clock Report*, they would grab a bite, then club through the night, but he had called with the out-of-the-blue news that he'd been traded to the L.A. Dodgers and had to be in the City of Angels for tomorrow's matinee game. So, since her publisher had been clamoring for her to finish the sequel to her bestseller, *Six O'Clock and the Single Girl*, she had hidden from her feelings by starting the next chapter.

She finished the paragraph she was on, all the while her mind lingering on the obvious: Paul was going to ask her to follow him to the left coast, and she was going to have to choose between him and her newly negotiated contract that made her one of the nation's highest-paid local anchors.

As she opened the door, she could tell her usually optimistic father was not his typical self. "Glad I caught you when you weren't doing anything," he said.

"Just playing on the computer," she said. "You know how we lonely old maids get at night."

"Don't worry, I won't tell Paul," said the Chief of Detectives. "Anyway," he said, throwing his suit coat over her new white leather couch, "I need to talk." He went straight to her fridge. "I can see by the Sam Adams that the person you never tell dear old dad about is still in the picture."

"Perceptive as ever," she said. Even though they lived within a few miles, her father rarely came by for a visit, except for two things. She wondered which one it was tonight. And then it hit her.

"I was expecting you, actually," she lied, irritated at herself for not being ready. Best to ease into things, she told herself. "The last time we talked, Dad, you were debating labeling the Strong case as cold. Made up your mind yet?"

Matt Locke pulled two long necks out and unscrewed their tops. "If you ever get tired of news reporting, you could start a new career as Madame Kelly, Mind Reader. He handed her a bottle, oblivious to the wineglass that sat beside her computer. "I'd hate to put that box in the storeroom. Any time the owner of a company involved in national defense is found dead in his office with a major gash in his skull, a lot of people want answers, but there are none."

"Nothing new?" tried Kelly.

"No new forensic evidence, no new witnesses, no new suspects, and no reason to doubt the interviews with his widow, his son, or even the butler."

Kelly sat down on the new couch across from her favorite Lazy-Boy that her father had appropriated. "A dead end."

"As dead as the last time we talked," he admitted, "but it's like watching your favorite movie over and over—you think you'll see something new or at least gain a different perspective than you used to have."

"Can I check out the evidence box?" Kelly said. "Since it's only 8:05 now, I'd guess you came here straight from work and have the box in your car's trunk because you're going to take just one more look at it."

"Remind me not to try to hide any birthday or Christmas presents from you," said the detective, taking a deep draw on the amber bottle. "Why is it that every time I come over here, I feel like a cross between Watson and Tonto?"

At that moment her cell phone buzzed, identifying the caller as her agent. "Excuse me, Dad. I have to grab this." She walked into her bedroom. "Fira, what's up?"

"Haveta hurry, girl. Taking a big meeting in an n-sec on *Kardasians: The Movie*," her agent fired out. "Best deal I can get you in L.A. on such short notice is weekend anchor at the market's #2. Seems like a big step backwards, but it's your call."

"L.A....weekend anchor," said Kelly, aware that flabbergasted did not begin to describe her confusion. Then the what-do-I-need-to-complete-this-puzzle piece came to her. "Paul—"

"What a coincidence, girl. He's ringing in right now on my other line. Did I tell you he wants me to negotiate a new deal with the Dodgers? Hey, if Jay Z can represent jocks, why not little old Fira?"

"Paul asked you to find me a new job?"

"Just before he pleaded with me to represent him now that he's the toast of the coast."

"But," Kelly protested, "I didn't ask—"

"I know. Ain't it wonderful? You love dumplings have been cooking together in the same wine for so long that he knows what you want without you even asking. Gotta run. Ciao."

Once she got past the image of being cooked in wine, Kelly realized she was furious, but as she returned to the living room, she noticed her father had that look on his face that said he might actually enjoy listening to country music. She touched his hand. "It's that time of year again, isn't it?"

"'In me thou seest the twilight of such day/As after sunset fadeth in the west'."

"Shakespeare," said Kelly.

"Your mother," returned her father. "Since she left me, every day has seemed like twilight."

Kelly knelt down beside her father. "I can remember so clearly Coach Ferguson dropping me off at the precinct house after my softball game. I wondered why he wasn't taking me to the Remaleys' where Myles and I were staying while you and Mom had—what did she call it—a weekend alone. Coach didn't say a word."

"I told Fergie it was my job to tell you and Myles. I...I...still can't believe that explosion. I'd just gone down the mountain to get the paper and some donuts. Fire department said it was the propane tank...something about a leak. But I'd just checked it. Maybe if—"

"Dad," said Kelly, "not all mysteries can be solved."

"Maybe not," he said gruffly, "but this one above all should have been. Sweetheart, her body was in pieces. If only I could kiss that heart-shaped birthmark on her cheek one more time. She called it her love tattoo."

Kelly took his shaking hand. "Would you like to just sit here for a bit?"

He wiped his eyes. "No time for tears. We need to go down to my car and get that evidence box that I can tell you're just dying to pore through."

II

As she pulled her recently-purchased Mini-Cooper into the parking garage at WBAK-TV, Kelly couldn't keep her mind focused on either of the dueling emotions that had been vying for her attention since the previous evening. The image of her father, a man who was usually so in control of the situation, trying to stay outwardly strong while she knew he was crumbling inside at those devastating memories, had her on the edge of tears, while at the same time Paul's presumptive call to her agent about jobs in L.A. had her gritting her teeth.

Kelly headed toward the elevator, determined to put both emotions on hold so that she could get herself ready for the newscast coming up in a couple of hours. She wondered if Paul had told anyone else about "their" plans. The thought of her boss learning that a move to the west coast was even a possibility sent shivers down her spine. Bill Phillips was not the easiest of men to work with in the best of circumstances. Fira fought hard to get her the new contract, and Phillips had not given in without a struggle. Now, it could be a whole new ballgame…so to speak.

The first face to greet Kelly as she stepped off the elevator was that of Chuck Mann, her co-anchor of *The Six O'Clock Report*. Before she could say hi, Chuck grabbed her by the shoulders and pulled her close. "Is it true, Kel? Tell me it's true," he said in a conspiratorial tone that would have made Deep Throat proud.

"What are you talking about?" she said, pulling free.

"Aren't you the sly one," Chuck continued, straightening his too-expensive-for-a-local-news-anchor tie. "Haggling with management over that new contract while you're planning an escape to the coast with Mr. Golden Glove."

Somebody else knew, Kelly thought. And if Chuck knew, the entire station knew or soon would. "Chuck," she said, giving him a look that meant she was deadly serious, "nothing has been settled except that Paul has been traded to the Dodgers."

"If you're worried about me, don't be. I know we make a great team, but, to tell the truth, I've been giving some serious thought to going solo. And if you leave, I'll be able to pitch some great ideas to Bill."

"Great ideas?"

"Sure," said Chuck. "That special series you've been doing this year—*Locked Up*—has been pretty successful, but for me, Kel, it's a little dull."

"What's dull about stories dealing with bringing criminals to justice?"

"Maybe it's that just-the-facts-ma'am-Joe-Friday delivery of yours, but I know people today want more drama, more pizzazz. I'm thinking some live ride-along footage and some undercover shots to spice things up."

Kelly was having trouble stifling a smile at the thought of her co-anchor dressed in anything but his designer blazer and slacks haunting the city's docks in search of a drug deal.

"The series title would say it all," beamed the now-on-a-roll Chuck. "Something like 'Mann Up' or 'Odd Mann Out' or 'Under the Mann Hole'."

Just then, Kelly spotted Phillips coming toward them...and he didn't look happy. "Chuck," she said, stepping around the now-frenetic newsman, "sounds promising; let's talk later."

"Miss Locke," said her boss, using his called-on-the-carpet appellation, "we need to talk—now!"

III

Kelly opened the door to her condo and dragged herself to the refrigerator, dropping her purse and kicking off her Jimmy Choos in the process. What a night, she thought as she pulled a cool bottle and unscrewed the cap. She had felt like a middle-schooler as she sat across the huge metal desk from her boss and listened to him read her the riot act concerning loyalty, career suicide, and anything else he could dredge up to make her feel guilty about a move west.

"But, Bill," she squeezed in when he finally took a breath, "I haven't made any decision about a move."

"You have only one decision, young lady, and that is to honor your new contract."

"But I haven't signed it yet."

Phillips's face reddened. "Now I get it. This is a ploy to leverage more money. Probably that barracuda of an agent. I thought we were going to come to blows several times during those negotiations."

"Money has nothing to do with this," Kelly said, holding her sometimes quick temper.

With that, her boss stood, and in a totally dismissive tone said, "You'd best think about your future and the dire consequences of hubris, Miss Locke."

Kelly stared at the half-empty bottle. "Paul," she said, exasperated. Why couldn't he just head for L.A. by himself and give her some time to think about their relationship? And why hadn't he realized by now that she had a mind of her own and didn't like others making decisions for her—especially such important ones?

She decided to escape her domestic travails by diving into that which she loved since she read her first Sherlock Holmes story—mystery. She pulled out the evidence box her dad left the night before. When she worried about his leaving official material with a civilian, Matt Locke had countered with the dual rationale that the case was about to be classified "cold" and that he was the top of the food chain as far as determining who got to look at the material.

She had just started to flip through some reports in a manila folder when her cell phone buzzed. It was Paul.

"Hey, babe," came the familiar voice. "Hope I'm not calling too late, but I had to tell you about my day."

"Paul, please don't call me babe. I—"

"Sure thing. Man, what a day! First time in Dodger blue, and I hit for the cycle. The fans went bananas. You're going to love it here, babe…I mean Kel."

Kelly measured her words. "I can't believe you told people I was following you to Los Angeles, even got Fira to scout out a job. Paul, I have a good job here, and Dad—"

"Come on, Kel. You're not Daddy's little girl any more. You have to cut those strings. Moving away from all that comfort will do wonders for you…for us."

"But, Paul," Kelly said sternly, "you don't get to make that decision for me."

"I thought we had an understanding."

Kelly's throat tightened. "You could have at least given me time to talk with Dad. He's going through a tough period right now."

"Babe, you can't waste your life worrying about him…he's a big boy. Now, when are you coming out?"

"I can't talk about this now," said Kelly. She clicked off the phone as a tear welled up in her eye.

IV

A restless night's sleep had done little for Kelly's mood. After Paul's call, she had fought the urge to sulk and had returned to the evidence box. She'd found nothing that immediately caught her eye—just the official reports, a few crime scene photos, and some interview notes from the officer on call and her dad.

She was pouring a second cup of coffee when her phone buzzed. This time it was Matt Locke.

"Hey, Dad."

"Hi, Kelly. Just called to apologize for the weepy act last night. It's just that—"

"You don't have to explain anything. I know how much you loved Mom."

"Listen, Kelly, I'm driving out to the cemetery, and I wondered if you'd like to go."

Kelly's throbbing head protested, but she quickly said, "Sure."

A s Matt and Kelly walked through the tall grass at the Pheasant Run Cemetery, Kelly realized that they hadn't said a word the entire 20-minute drive.

Arriving at her mother's grave, Kelly tenderly squeezed her dad's huge hand. "You two really loved each other, didn't you?"

"It's hard to put into words. Twenty-eight years of total devotion."

"Wait a minute, Dad," said Kelly, releasing his hand. "You two were married twenty-nine years when she died."

Matthew Locke looked intently at the gravestone. "Libby," he said, "we agreed not to tell the kids."

"Tell us about what?"

Her dad turned to Kelly. "Your mother and I were going through a rough period when she died. That's why we were at the cabin. Thought maybe if we spent some time alone, we could set things right."

"Set things right?"

"Kelly, I was moving up in the force, lots of late nights and hurried meals. You and Myles were a handful to say the least, and your mother was feeling a bit deserted. We had you two rather late in our marriage, and she needed me to help out. I thought we were getting back on track that weekend, then…"

Kelly wrapped her arms around the bear of a man. "Dad, you can't blame yourself; it was an accident."

"That's just it, Kelly; for twenty-one years I've never believed your mother's death was an accident. I was supposed to be in that cabin, too. That explosion was meant for me."

V

Matt Locke guided the unmarked sedan into a parking slot at Rachel's, his newly-discovered best-restaurant-nobody's-heard-of, and turned off the engine. The drive from the cemetery had been as silent as the trip there.

"The least I can do," said Kelly's dad, "is treat you to an early lunch."

"Dad," said Kelly, again touching his hand, "we need to talk about what happened and why you think that explosion was meant for you."

Matt opened the door and pulled away. "Later, Kelly; now just isn't the time."

As they walked toward the restaurant, Kelly decided not to push things. She'd learned long ago that her dad had his own timetable for everything and nothing could make him change it. "I looked through the Strong evidence box last night. Nothing stuck out."

"Oh," said her dad, regaining some of his usual energy. "And I was so sure that like the Great Detective, you'd spot something that everyone else missed."

"Maybe if you'd review the case for me," said Kelly as they slid into the booth's bright red vinyl seats, "I'd be inspired."

Matt Locke chuckled and took a sip of water. "My notes pretty much tell it all. D. MacMillan Strong, one of our city's most powerful industrialists, was found dead in his study. As far as we could make out, someone hit him from behind with a brick from a display commemorating the opening of his first munitions plant way back in the 70s. The blood trail suggested that he tried to make it to the door, but fell as he passed a bookcase."

"Yeah," said Kelly. "I saw the shots of the body with the books he'd knocked off. By the way, who found him?"

"His wife, Beth. They'd been married thirty-eight years. She said she'd come to the study to remind him of a dinner engagement."

"How did she take his death?" questioned Kelly.

Matt put down the menu he'd been poring over. "Come to think of it, she was actually pretty cool for someone who's found a spouse murdered in such a brutal fashion."

"Did you think she was a possible suspect?"

"Not really. To tell the truth, she's a small person, and I'm not sure she could have handled that brick. Besides, she had just returned home from a charity event downtown. Had three credible witnesses."

Kelly glanced at the menu. "Any suggestions?"

"They have a cook here named Chris, who makes a killer—pardon the pun—lasagna. In fact, when we walked in, they probably assumed we'd be having it."

"Lasagna it is," said Kelly, closing the menu. "You said you interviewed a son."

"Yeah, only child. Russell was the apple of his father's eye, according to all accounts. Sent to the best schools and groomed to take over Strong Industries."

"You know what they say about murders and close relatives."

"My interviews with those closest to the family admitted that Russell and his father crossed swords at times over how the business should be run—the old man was old school while Russell was more 21st Century in his approach—but at the end of the day, they seemed to be genuinely close. That day, Russell was across town at the family stables. Seems he was quite the polo player."

Kelly interrupted her inquiry long enough to take a bite of the steaming lasagna placed before her. "Wow! I can see why you hesitate to order anything else—this is terrific."

"Told you," said Matt.

Even the mouthwatering dish couldn't keep Kelly quiet for long. "Did Strong have any enemies?"

"I might be able to name friends more quickly. Face it, this guy was a successful businessman who didn't mind stepping on people to get what he wanted, so, yes, he had enemies."

"Did any seem capable of murder?"

Matt wiped the corner of his mouth. "To tell the truth, they all seemed plenty capable, but I have my eye on three guys in particular."

"And they would be?"

"Anton Spasky, a Russian immigrant who runs an import-export business and was Strong's chief competition to buy the Metros—"

"Paul's team." Kelly didn't want to introduce the issue of Paul's leaving, since her dad seemed to be one of the few who didn't know.

"That's right. Those two have been jockeying for months."

"But to kill someone over a baseball team?"

"Hey, sports are big business. George Steinbrenner bought the Yankees for $10 million in 1973, and today Forbes tells us they're worth $1.3 billion. I've worked cases where someone was killed for a pack of cigarettes."

"You said you had three major suspects."

"That's right." Matt signaled the server for some coffee. "Number two is Cotton Hazelwood, Strong's chief rival for a massive contract with the military for unmanned drones. The company that gets the contract will probably put the other out of business or at least eliminate its ability to seriously compete in the future."

"And the third?" said Kelly swirling the cream into her cup.

"He's the strangest of them all. Glenn Hall."

"Chopper Hall, the Kingmaker?"

"Bingo." Matt took a sip of the steaming coffee. "He got the name Chopper for all the political assassinations he's carried out over the years."

"What connection did he have with Strong?"

"His real connection was with Russell. He was convinced that Russell was the next John Kennedy Jr., and he was angling to get Russell into politics."

"But what makes him a suspect in Strong the elder's murder?"

Kelly's dad took another drink of his undoctored coffee. "The old man was grooming Russell to take over the business. The last thing he wanted was for his son to detour into politics. Your station probably covered that dust-up Strong had with Hall last year at the Dewey Charity Ball. Strong called Hall a parasite, and Hall grabbed him and threatened to crush him if Strong didn't back off."

"From what?"

"Everybody assumed he meant his attempts to push Russell into the political arena."

Kelly drained her cup. "That's quite a rogues's gallery. I'd say you're right in your estimate that any of the three would be capable of murder."

"But singling out the murderer hasn't been as easy. As you might suspect with men of such wealth and influence, they all had alibis for the time of the murder. Thus my stone wall."

As her dad called for the bill, Kelly quickly ran over a couple of scenarios in her mind. Like her favorite detective, she let the pieces swirl until she could fit them into their proper order. She didn't have everything she needed yet, but the conversation had been a start.

"By the way, Kelly, will you and Paul be coming by for dinner this weekend? I've ordered some steaks from Omaha, and I can't wait to try out that new grill."

Kelly froze. She didn't have the energy to launch into her current romantic dilemma. "Can't make it, Dad; Paul's got a road game."

VI

Kelly picked up the autographed baseball from her freshly dusted desk. As she ran her fingers over the seams, she remembered the night she had gotten it from Paul. The Metros were playing the Red Sox and holding on to a 3–1 lead in the ninth. The bases were loaded when David Ortiz hit a drive to center field. The Metros's all-star center fielder turned and headed right at her as she held her breath. Not three feet from the fence he held up his glove and made a leaping catch over his shoulder to end the game.

As the crowd went wild, the player looked at her before pitching her the ball and inviting her to meet him outside the locker room. That night Paul would not only take her to dinner but also return the ball to her after having it signed by the entire team.

She pitched the ball into the air. What a whirlwind romance they had. She was used to cameras, but being with a celebrity was an entirely different story. Everywhere they went, photographers popped out of nowhere to snap pictures, and fans of all ages ignored any sense of privacy to clamor for an autograph on a program, a menu, or, more than once, a part of the feminine anatomy.

Suddenly the door burst open, interrupting Kelly's reverie. The long-legged woman in a tight, almost-too-short skirt leaped toward the desk.

"Fira," blurted out Kelly.

"The one and only. Girl, I just couldn't wait to give you the news."

"Dare I ask what news?"

Fira's flawless coffee-colored face lit up even more than usual. "When WSEE, L.A.'s numero uno station, heard that number two made a contract offer to you and took a look at your tapes—courtesy of yours truly—they couldn't wait to make a counter offer. Girl, we're L.A.-bound!"

Kelly replaced the baseball on its stand. "Wait just a minute, Fira. Did it ever occur to you that I might not want to go the West Coast?"

"Who isn't California dreaming? You and Paul—and I've decided to represent our favorite center fielder. I've got such plans for the two of you. Brad and Angelina, Kanye and Kim, Paul and Kelly."

"Sounds like everybody has plans for me." Kelly stood up. "Moving is a big decision, and I don't want to be rushed into anything."

"Rushed?" said her agent. "The station's given us till Monday for an answer."

"Considering this is Thursday, I'd say rushed pretty much covers it."

Fira placed her hands on her hips in exasperation. "Girl, I just worked my young butt off for you, and now you're telling me you need time to think about things?"

"'Fraid so."

"Well, you're throwing away a big score, but like I said, it's your life. And what about Paul? He assumed—"

"You know what they say about assume." Kelly took the baseball from its stand again, but this time she dropped it into a desk drawer.

VII

Kelly and her dad stood in front of the large oak door at the Strong's mansion. Kelly convinced the Chief of Detectives that another interview with the widow might prove helpful. If Mrs. Strong told the entire truth, perhaps she would remember something she missed during her period of grief, and, if she lied, perhaps she would slip up and contradict her earlier account.

"I'm surprised," said Kelly as they waited, "that there were no security cameras here the day of the murder."

"I told you Strong was old school…said his privacy was important and he didn't want a bunch of cameras recording his every move."

The door opened, and an older man in a white shirt and vest led them to a sitting room. Just as they were refusing an offer of something to drink, a beautiful lady with silver hair and immaculate make-up glided into the room.

"Mrs. Strong," said Kelly's dad, as he stood.

"Chief...ah...Locke, isn't it?" she said with an easy smile. "Please be seated...and introduce me to your charming companion." She took a seat across an ornate coffee table from them, straightening what Kelly recognized as a Vera Wang original.

"This is my daughter, Kelly. She's a news person, and I thought she might provide some new insight into your husband's death."

"Poor David," said Beth Strong, "in some ways his death seems so long ago and yet just yesterday." She dropped her eyes momentarily. "I just don't see what help I can be; I've told you all I know about that horrible day."

"Mrs. Strong," said Kelly. "I'm more interested in your husband's company." Since her earlier discussion with her dad, Kelly zeroed in on the murder weapon. Was it a weapon of opportunity, or did it hold some significance for the killer?

"Strong Industries was the brainchild of David and his best friend, Mason Mitchell. They grew up together, and even though David was of wealthy parents, while Mason's family was of meager means, they were like brothers."

"I don't recall meeting a Mason Mitchell," said Matt Locke.

"Oh, no," Beth Strong said. "Poor Mason died years ago while on a business trip to Thailand."

"So Mitchell helped found the company," said Kelly.

"During those early years," said Mrs. Strong, "some held that David was the money behind the venture while Mason was the brains." The widow looked toward the ceiling-to-floor window across the room. "Mason's death rocked us all."

"Exactly when did he die?" asked Kelly.

"In 1975. Our company was barely three years old at the time."

Matt Locke fingered the pages of a small notebook he pulled from his jacket pocket. "Didn't you and Mr. Strong marry that same year?"

"I've always wondered if David and I ran to each other out of sorrow in the loss of such a dear friend." Her eyes seemed to dampen a bit. "In any case, ours became a strong marriage that withstood the years."

"Mother." The trio looked toward the doorway to see a tall, muscular man, who Kelly thought could have stepped from the red carpet in Hollywood. "Howard told me we had guests."

"Chief Locke, I believe you remember my son, Russell," said Beth Strong. "Russell, let me introduce you to Chief Locke's daughter, Kelly."

The fortyish man nodded toward Matt. "Chief Locke." As he walked behind his seated mother, Russell Strong looked directly at Kelly. "Ms. Locke, haven't I seen you on one of our local television stations?"

"I do the six o'clock news for Channel 4."

"Chief Locke and his daughter came out for some additional information concerning your father's death," said Beth Strong, glancing over her shoulder.

Russell Strong grimaced. "I'm not sure what else we can say. Chief Locke, have you made any headway?"

"I'm not at liberty to go into detail, but every day brings us a bit closer to a solution," Matt lied.

"Mr. Strong," Kelly interjected, "I guess you're now running Strong Industries."

"That's what David always wanted," Beth Strong said quickly.

"And what about your political career?" asked Kelly, remembering her earlier discussion with her dad.

Russell Strong seemed a little off balance. "How did you know—"

"We news people keep our ears to the ground," said Kelly.

"Well," said the younger Strong, "I have been putting out some feelers." He looked down at his mother. "But as always the business comes first."

Kelly thought she'd shake things up a bit. "Would Glenn Hall agree with that sentiment?"

Russell Strong's face flushed ever so slightly.

"Chief Locke, have we given you the additional information you desire?" said Beth Strong, rising abruptly and turning toward the door.

Matt Locke looked at Kelly as they rose. "I guess we have what we need."

As they walked toward their car, Kelly asked, "How old would you say Russell Strong is?"

"Don't have to guess on that one; he's thirty-eight."

"Looks like 1975 was quite an important year for the Family Strong," said Kelly, fitting a couple more pieces into the puzzle.

VIII

Matt Locke's sedan pulled up in front of the Municipal Building downtown. "Hall's office said he'd be in meetings till 11:00," said Kelly's dad, "so I thought we could catch him here."

Kelly relished the chance to talk with Chopper Hall, but realized that she needed to get to the station to prepare for The Six O'Clock Report. After all, detective work was a sideline, and with her boss on the warpath, she wanted to assure her paycheck was not in danger.

As they exited the car, Kelly caught a glimpse of a short, shaved-headed figure coming down the steps of the columned building. She immediately thought of Michael Chicklis, one of her favorite television actors.

Matt Locke intercepted Hall before the suited figure could reach his limo. "Mr. Hall," he said.

Glenn Hall waved off the huge driver, who was rounding the car in security mode. "Chief Locke, what can I do for the city's finest today?"

"A couple of questions about the Strong murder," said Kelly's dad.

"I thought we were finished with all that," said Hall. "Besides, I was not even in town when the tragedy occurred."

"A man's dead, and I intend to find his killer," said Matt.

Hall noticed Kelly as she emerged from behind her dad. "And you are?"

"Kelly Locke," said Kelly.

"My daughter," said Matt.

"Look, Chief," said Hall, "I have a full schedule today, so if you have a question, ask it…quickly."

Kelly stepped in front of her dad. "Mr. Hall, we understand that you've been advising Russell Strong on a possible political career and that his father was not very pleased."

"So?" said Hall.

"Didn't you two have a little push-and-shove awhile back at the Dewey Ball?" asked Kelly.

"Nothing I haven't done with any number of people with whom I had a difference of opinion. Look, Strong and I didn't get along, but if anything, he had reason to kill me. Russell agreed to throw his hat in the ring for state senator. The last thing I wanted was for the old man to leave the business for his son to run. Now Russell's getting cold feet and spouting his mantra, 'The business comes first.'"

"Mr. Hall," said Matt, "thanks for your time."

As the driver opened the limo door, Hall turned to Matt Locke. "If I were you, I'd have a chat with Cotton Hazelwood. You know he and Strong were struggling to get that government contract for drone production, and my Washington contacts tell me that one of them leaked some information that had the Senate ready to open an investigation."

IX

Kelly shuffled through the papers on her desk as she tried to pull herself together for the newscast coming up in a little over an hour. She and her dad had been unsuccessful in their afternoon attempt to see Cotton Hazelwood, who was in London and wouldn't return till the middle of the week.

On a hunch, she had placed a call to her brother, Myles, who was what some would call a "Washington Insider." She hoped his behind-closed-door contacts could open some doors for her. Of course, she'd gotten the familiar leave-a-message response to her call, and knowing her brother, a response might never come.

She was skipping between thoughts of the Strong case and her own career and romantic dilemmas when her phone buzzed. "Kelly Locke," she answered.

"Sis," came the familiar voice. "Just got your message."

"Myles, this sets the record for speed of response from you. Been playing any football lately?" asked Kelly, remembering a video she had seen of her brother enjoying the benefits of the high-tech advances she helped him acquire a few months earlier.

"Look, Sis, I realize I wasn't exactly forthcoming with you about that technology and why I needed it, but be happy for me. I couldn't walk unassisted before, and next month I'll be running a marathon. I owe it all to my little sister."

"Did you get a chance to look into my situation?"

"Didn't have to. When it comes to things military, your big brother is always on the need-to-know A list."

"So what about Strong and Hazelwood?" Kelly asked. "Did one of them leak damaging information on the other?"

"Whoever told you that had his wires crossed. In fact, Strong and Hazelwood were in the process of combining resources in order to fill the drone order from the military. All this is hush-hush, but those two needed each other. With Strong gone, the whole deal is in jeopardy."

"So you don't think Hazelwood had a motive to kill his old rival?"

"Far from it. Why do you think he's in London as we speak? He's hedging his bets, trying to form a coalition of smaller manufacturers to replace Strong Industries if the new Strong management backs out of the deal."

"You've been very helpful, Myles, and I don't think it'll cost me anything this time."

"You've grown so cynical, Sis. But seriously, I hope you and Dad can forgive me for my less-than-honest behavior."

"Your help with this case is certainly a step in the right direction."

As she clicked off her phone, Kelly thought, two down and one to go.

X

Kelly and her dad stepped off the elevator on the tenth floor of the downtown office tower. The night before, she made it through her newscast with Chuck Mann uneventfully, successfully avoided Bill Phillips, and sent a call from Paul to voice mail. Now, after her first good night's sleep in days, her mind was clear, and she wanted to collect a few more pieces of the puzzle.

The duo stepped through the door marked Spasky Import-Export. The young receptionist looked up from her computer screen. "May I help you?"

"Chief Matthew Locke to see Mr. Spasky," Kelly's dad said in his most official voice.

The receptionist walked down a carpeted hall, then returned and ushered Kelly and her dad back to a large office adorned with what looked like original oil paintings and bronze sculptures.

"Chief Locke, we meet again," said the hulking figure in a finely-tailored pinstripe suit. He held out a hand even larger than Matt's. "Do I see a resemblance?" he continued, looking at Kelly.

"My daughter, Kelly."

"I trust your visit has something to do with my old friend's death."

"Just a few more questions," said Matt.

"Fire away," he said, chuckling at his cleverness.

"Mr. Spasky," said Kelly, "we understand that you and the late Mr. Strong were in conflict over the possible ownership of the Metros."

"Chief Locke, has your lovely daughter decided to follow in your footsteps in law enforcement?"

Before Matt could speak, Kelly continued, "With Mr. Strong no longer in the picture, the field is open, so to speak, for you."

"My dear, the field was open, as you put it, long before his untimely death. Records will reveal that my old friend bowed out of the competition well before he left this earth."

"And why was that?" said Matt.

"Let's just say the two of us had a long history, and he ended his pursuit of the team as a personal favor to me."

"My read on Strong is that he wasn't much into personal favors," said Matt.

"It's no secret that many years ago my old friend was instrumental in helping me immigrate from my native Russia and set up what has become a highly successful business. To harm such a benefactor would be a betrayal of all principle."

"It seems as if your friendship with Mr. Strong was sort of unbalanced," said Kelly. "He seemed to do the giving and you, the taking."

Spasky sat down on the corner of his mammoth oak desk. "While I feel no real obligation to explain my friendship, I shall as one last thank-you to my old colleague. In the mid-70's, 1975 to be exact, the newly-established Strong Industries sent a young executive named Mason Mitchell to Cambodia to negotiate a deal. At the time I was stationed there with the Soviet military. As you know, Cambodia was an extremely hostile place for Americans at the time, a place no individual with ties to the American war machine should have been. To make a rather lengthy story digestible, the executive, who was also the close friend of Mr. Strong, came into harm's way. While I was ultimately unsuccessful in my attempt to protect him, Mr. Strong later rewarded my efforts with his, shall we call it, sponsorship."

"So Mason Mitchell was killed in Cambodia?" said Kelly.

"Unfortunately," said Spasky. "As I told Strong and his son shortly before his death, that arms deal he was working on with the Hazelwood group, like any venture of such magnitude, could have unintended consequences."

As Kelly and her dad headed back to the ground floor, the puzzle was coming into sharper focus. Unintended consequences indeed, she thought. But she still had a few pieces to arrange.

XI

Matt Locke had been a bit hesitant to revisit the Strong mansion, but Kelly assured him that the trip would be worthwhile. Since the first time she had looked at the crime scene photos, something stuck in her mind: the books on the floor.

"Kelly," said her dad, as Howard once again answered the door, "I hope this isn't a wild goose chase."

"I just need to see Strong's study."

This time Beth Strong met them at the door. Again, she was dressed for the fashion runway in a floral gown with all the accessories. "Chief Locke, do I need to charge you rent?"

Kelly took the lead. "Mrs. Strong, we need to see your husband's study."

"Well, I guess there would be no harm. Come this way."

The trio walked through several rooms straight out of *Architectural Digest* till they arrived at a large room lined with windows. "We haven't been in here since that terrible day," said Beth Strong.

Kelly walked immediately to a large bookcase between the door and the roll-top desk that dominated the far wall. "Dad, you said your theory on why Mr. Strong was found over here when he was struck at his desk was that he attempted to make it to the door to call for help."

"That's right."

"When I saw the crime scene photos and noticed only a few books on the floor, I wondered if maybe he wasn't headed for the door, but for the bookcase."

"What in the world for?" said Beth Strong.

Kelly ran her fingers over the books. Three seemed out of place according to the simple historical arrangement.

"After the techs removed the body, they just stuck the books back in the case. I should have considered them possible evidence, but as you often say, Kelly, even Homer nods."

One large book caught Kelly's eye. The Works of John Dryden. As she pulled it from the shelf, she noticed a dark stain on the spine. Probably dried blood.

"What do you make of all this?" Matt asked.

"That semester in English Lit wasn't a complete waste," said Kelly. "Dryden gave us a very famous poem that has a particular relevance to this case."

"And that would be?" questioned Matt.

"Absalom and Achitophel," said Kelly. "It's a narrative poem about the Biblical struggles between King David and his beloved son Absalom."

Beth Strong steadied herself with the back of a leather wing chair.

Matt Locke looked at the now-pale widow. "Are you saying—"

"Mr. Strong left us a dying clue. In both the Biblical and Dryden's accounts, David is indirectly responsible for his son's death, but I think Mr. Strong's intent was clear."

Beth Strong collapsed into the chair, hands covering her face.

"What's going on in here?" said Russell Strong, entering the room.

"Oh, Russell," blurted out his mother, "they know."

Russell Strong's body stiffened. "Mother."

Kelly held out the centuries-old volume. "I'd say your father told us, but that wouldn't be exactly true, would it, Russell?"

"I'm not sure I'm following all this, Kelly," said Matt.

Kelly looked at a sobbing Beth Strong. "Secrets can be deadly, and the longer they go untold, the worse the situation can become."

Russell Strong bristled. "I think you two should leave. Clearly, you're upsetting my mother." He put his hands on Beth Strong's shoulders.

"Dad," said Kelly. "It took me a while and some help from an old mentor of mine, but I think I've finally put the pieces together. Mr. Strong's murder had its roots in the 70s even before his marriage to Mrs. Strong."

As Kelly spoke, Russell Strong crouched in front of his mother, his head almost in her lap.

"Wealthy David Strong and brilliant Mason Mitchell started a munitions company just as the Vietnam War heated up. Things between the friends were solid, except for one thorn—both men loved the same woman."

Beth Strong let out a muffled sob as Russell stroked her silver hair.

"When we first talked with Mrs. Strong, I sensed some tension when she mentioned those early years and Mitchell."

Matt Locke shifted his weight. "But how did that lead—"

"It was during our chat with Anton Spasky that the picture started to clear for me. In fact, after talking with Mr. Spasky, I went home and pulled out one of my favorite Holmes collections—the original 24 stories from *The Strand Magazine*."

"Look, Kelly," Matt said, "I know that sometimes you channel the Great Detective to help you with mysteries, but…"

"With Spasky's account of Mason Mitchell's death, I couldn't help but see some parallels between this situation and the one in Holmes' 'Adventure of the Crooked Man.' In Doyle's story, an army sergeant sends one of his men on a suicide mission in order to eliminate him as a rival for the love of a beautiful woman."

"Sounds like another episode in the Biblical David's life," said Matt Locke. "I remember the story of his sending Uriah off to be killed so that he could have Uriah's wife, Bathsheba."

"Your memory is good, Dad," said Kelly. "In fact, Doyle alluded to that Biblical tale in his story."

With that, Beth Strong collapsed into her son's arms, sobbing uncontrollably.

"Earlier," continued Kelly, "Mrs. Strong said that Mitchell died in Thailand, doubtless what David Strong had told her all those years ago."

Matt Locke frowned. "But Spasky said he was killed in Cambodia, a place hostile to Americans."

"And Russell heard that contradictory information," said Kelly. "My guess is he told his mother about Strong's earlier dangerous dealings in order to get her to talk Strong into nixing what Spasky called another dangerous deal with Hazelwood, a deal Russell proved to be against."

Russell Strong pulled away from his mother. "Chief Locke, your daughter should go into fiction writing rather than newscasting. What a story. Now, I must insist that you leave."

Matt Locke stood his ground. "Your mother doesn't seem to think Kelly's spinning a yarn."

"And there's more to this true story, isn't there, Mrs. Strong?" said Kelly.

Beth Strong rose to her feet, trying hard to compose herself. "Russell, the lies end here. For thirty-eight years, this family has rested on untruths, and I say it ends—today."

"Mother, please," said Russell Strong.

"When Russell told me about Mason and Cambodia, everything became clear. David sent his best friend to Southeast Asia to die. Then the door opened for him to once again pursue me. Yes, David knew that as long as Mason was alive, my heart belonged to him."

"But there was something he didn't know, never knew even when he died," said Kelly.

Beth Strong grabbed her son. "Everybody wondered why I agreed to marry David so soon after Mason's death and the grief it caused."

"Russell is Mason's son," said Kelly.

"We were in love, even though we had no real plans for marriage," said Beth Strong. "David never knew. I had to make him believe Russell was his in order to protect a piece of Mason. Even though our marriage was loveless, I had to keep up appearances."

Kelly realized that Beth Strong's deception was made easier back then since DNA testing was not yet available. "And Russell never knew," said Kelly, "until your conversation about Cambodia and Mason Mitchell's death."

Beth Strong drew in a deep breath. "I was so hurt, so angry. David caused Mason's death, then lied to me all these years."

Kelly looked at her dad. "When Russell learned the truth of his parentage, he went into a rage. The man he looked up to all these years had in effect murdered his real father. And how appropriate to use a piece of the factory Strong and Mitchell built as the weapon of his revenge. The dying clue suggests that Russell didn't reveal what he knew and that David Strong died believing his killer was the son he loved."

Matt Locke walked toward a slumping Russell Strong as Beth Strong covered her eyes.

XII

Matt Locke flipped the New York strips on the grill as he whistled the theme from *The Magnificent Seven*, his all-time favorite movie. "Kelly, I can't tell you how great it felt to move that evidence box to the Closed Case file."

Kelly was busy setting the table across the patio. "This case was a tough one, and even though we closed it, I can't help feeling bad, especially for Beth Strong."

Kelly's dad stopped whistling. "Relationships between men and women can be touchy. Love, honesty, distrust…all those emotions come into play. It's always a balancing act, one of give and take."

As her dad went back to grilling, Kelly thought about her relationship with Paul. Why did she ever think it would work? Compromise was not in Paul's vocabulary—unless it was defined as "you give me what I want."

"Too bad Paul couldn't be with us tonight," said Matt. "I know he'd love these steaks."

"Dad," said Kelly, "Paul's sort of…out of the picture."

"Out of the picture?"

"When you read tomorrow's sports page, look at the box score for the L.A. Dodgers and you'll see a familiar name. Paul was traded…and he wanted me to go with him to the coast."

Matt Locke put down his tongs. "And?"

"Well, I'm just not ready for that move geographically or emotionally. Besides, for all his wailing and gnashing of teeth, Mr. Phillips caved on Fira's demands and upped the terms of my new contract."

"Sweetheart, you know I want what's best for you, but you gotta believe I'm one happy guy that you'll be staying. If you left, who would listen to my stale jokes and help me solve crimes?"

Kelly laughed as she placed a plate of sliced tomatoes on the table.

Suddenly, Matt grew solemn. "Your mother would be so proud of you. She was such an independent soul, and you're just like her. Kelly, I miss her more every day."

Kelly walked across the patio and hugged her dad. "Don't worry; you can't get rid of me—even if the steaks are burned."

Matt quickly pulled the smoking slabs of meat from the grill and threw them on a platter. "Oh, before we eat, I want you to see something in today's paper—front page news about Cotton Hazelwood and that drone deal. The paper's on the chair."

Kelly retrieved the newspaper as her dad took the steaks to the table. Something caught her eye in a picture above the fold on the exposed social section. She swallowed hard before heading for the table. "Dad!"

Kelly handed the paper to her dad and pointed at the photo. In the corner of a picture taken at a society ball in Miami stood an elderly brunette woman whose profile revealed a heart-shaped birthmark on her left cheek.

✗

CLOSING THE CIRCLE

By Sergio Gaut vel Hartman

Translated from the Spanish by Lewis Shiner

"**A**fternoon. Remember me?"

The man interfering with Colonel Iribarren's walk was short, dark-complexioned, curly-haired, dressed in an aviator's jacket, canvas pants, and leather boots.

"No," Iribarren said. "Should I?"

"I think so." He took a cigarette out of his inside jacket pocket, and it looked to Iribarren as if he lit it with some kind of magical pass of the same hand. "You killed me."

Iribarren stopped. Twilight was passing into night. He looked up at the clearing sky and the moon rising between the buildings along the avenue. "Ah, yes. I don't remember you in particular, but I killed several like you. They don't usually come back to complain. Are you sure it was me?"

"You that killed me, or you that gave the order?"

"Either one," Iribarren said casually. Dealing with a pathological liar didn't seem much worse than some of the other tough situations he'd been in during his long life.

"Maybe you'd remember if I told you my name."

"I doubt it," Iribarren said, losing patience.

"In life I was Comandante Sampedro."

Iribarren took a step to the side, intending to walk around him and not waste any more time. Considering the weirdness of the situation, he thought he'd handled himself well, not giving in to his usual hostility or cynicism. So when this so-called Comandante Sampedro mirrored him and again blocked his way, he'd had enough.

"Excuse me. Alive or dead, you are holding me up. My family is waiting for me. I don't know you and I had nothing to do with your death, so I will ask you, politely, to get out of my way."

"Get out of my way" came out an octave higher than the rest of the sentence. At that moment, the streetlights of the Reconciliation National Park all came on at once. It was like a lightning bolt that refused to fade away.

Iribarren flinched, and Sampedro smiled. Behind Sampedro he could now see a multitude of men and women, children and old people, their faces somber and tense.

"Pick one, Colonel. If you didn't kill me, I'm sure that you killed some of these people, maybe quite a few of them—though one, just as an example, should suffice, don't you think?"

Iribarren's face, pale as the moon, showed that this time Sampedro had gotten through to him. This crowd was calling him to account, him in particular. Dead or alive, there they were. Real or not, there they were. He would not, however, make the obvious excuse that he was only following orders. True to his style, he counterattacked.

"I remember one or two. Somebody named Bernal? Rosa Naranjo, Bernardo Zelinsky, and a boy they used to call Metralla, Marcelo Cardoso. Are they somewhere in there?" He waved his hand at them. "Is that enough for you?"

"They are," Sampedro said with great seriousness. "Yes, it's enough."

Four figures moved out of the crowd to stand on either side of Sampedro. The woman held a little girl by the hand. Zelinsky was a decrepit old man and Metralla and Bernal were barely adolescents.

"Are you the ones I named?" Iribarren said. "I don't remember your faces."

"Selective memory," Sampedro said. "It's better to forget some things—especially the faces of the people you kill."

Iribarren was unmoved. "And now? You want revenge?"

The five looked at each other, and finally the woman, Rosa, spoke. "Do you think we wouldn't do it? We would tear you to pieces without shame or regret. But we can't. The dead can't kill."

"Ah," Iribarren said. "The dead can't kill."

"You're not afraid?" Bernal asked. Now he seemed to be a calm and ordinary man, not a boy, much less the sort of hallucination that you could squash like a cockroach.

"Afraid of a nightmare?" Iribarren nearly smiled.

"So that's it," Sampedro said. "You think you're dreaming." He bit his lip; Iribarren guessed he hadn't counted on having to prove his own existence.

"I'm either dreaming or hallucinating," Iribarren insisted. "It must have started when you crossed my path, though I don't seem to remember what happened before that. My memories are quite clear up to a point, then there's an abyss. But there's one thing I'm certain of, and that's that you are all a creation of my mind. You don't exist."

"Of your injured mind? Of your sick mind?" Sampedro was lashing out in attempt to get his momentum back, but Iribarren knew himself to be hard, very hard. A phantom of a dead man had no power over him.

"Of my mind."

"What are you trying to say?" Zelinsky took a step forward and extended one arm. He had enormous hands and could have strangled Iribarren with just one of them. "Do you think you can get out of this by pleading insanity?"

"I don't believe in ghosts," Iribarren said. "Nor do I believe in guilt, nor in myths, nor in grief. The one thing I believe in, a little, is death."

"And that's why you think you're dreaming," Sampedro said.

Iribarren shrugged. "There's no other explanation. I only have to try and I'll wake up. I've done it before." He squeezed his eyelids shut, making lines like a musical staff across his forehead, with two or three warts and a scar composing a melody there. But when he opened his eyes again, the scene had not changed. For the first time he felt a little disoriented.

"Distorted or not," Sampedro said, "the vision persists. So what other explanation is there? What's left? Maybe something of the abyss, of the black night?"

"I don't understand what you're saying. Maybe I've fallen into a drug-induced trance. That's possible. Somebody gave me a drug to force me to live through this experience. But it can't last forever. It will pass."

Comandante Sampedro snorted. "It's much worse than you think. No, Colonel, what we've built for you is not a nightmare, it's more like a prison, and you'll stay there forever. We've made sure there's no escape for you."

"I will escape," Iribarren said calmly. "Don't be stupid. I'll wake up." He paused to take out a cigarette. He didn't know any magic tricks, so he lit it with a match. He blew out a mouthful of smoke and pointed to Sampedro with the cigarette. It shook a little. "I will tell you that I've about had it with this dream. You are all dead, and well dead, my men and I made sure of that. So I'm going to charge right through you, and you will all disappear like the smoke from this cigarette."

"What if we're not made of fog?" Zelinsky said. "Then you're in real trouble, aren't you?"

Iribarren saw that what the dead man said was true; he had to charge into the wall to see what it was made of.

"Why don't you just accept your fate quietly?" Sampedro said. "Did it never occur to you that you would have to pay for what you did?"

Iribarren did not resist the wave of laughter that rose up within him. "Punishment? Do you think that we did what we did to spend the rest of our lives waiting to be punished? For the very will that gave strength to our hands? We know how to recognize when God is moving through our veins, mixed with our blood. Maybe you didn't have the will to kill us?"

The frozen scene, with the dead and the killer facing each other like pieces on a chessboard, suddenly came to life. The Reconciliation National Park turned into a barren wasteland of a battlefield. One single throat—the multitude united—howled a pure and piercing scream and Iribarren could not keep himself from shivering.

"No, we didn't lack the will," Sampedro said.

"And we don't lack it now," said Zelinsky, shaking his fist centimeters from Iribarren's nose.

Iribarren snapped his eyes open and the dead retreated.

"You're nothing," he said. "Smoke, fog, vapor, a condensation of my own doubts. But I will not let myself feel guilty for what I did, for what we did."

"We're evenly matched, Iribarren," said Sampedro, moving back to his former position. "But we have held back a small advantage, microscopic. Do you play chess?"

"Where did that come from? Yes, I play, what of it?"

"You will know, then, that a good player is able to see the moves that will lead him to victory even in the heart of the most frozen stalemate. Symmetry and balance."

"Leave me in peace! Is this your vengeance, keeping me here against my will, tormenting me with riddles and veiled threats?"

Sampedro laughed, and some of the others joined in, without much conviction. "You buy for nothing and want to sell for a fortune. No, Iribarren, it would be too dull for us to settle for having you live through this as no more than a nightmare."

"It is a nightmare, damn you! I'm going to wake up and all of you will melt into nothing."

"It's not a nightmare, Colonel," said Rosa.

"It's not a nightmare," echoed Bernal.

"Are you going to repeat it a thousand times, 'it's not a nightmare, it's not a nightmare,' do you think that'll be enough?" A cynical look stained Iribarren's face. "On top of being dead, you're all imbeciles. You can't act this way. I'm a professional, I know what I did was right. I'd do it again. Do you think you're the only ones with ideals, with values?"

"A minute ago you said you didn't believe in guilt, or in grief, which made me think you don't believe in much of anything," Sampedro said. "Except, a little, in death. You said that yourself, not me. Now you talk about ideals, values…"

"Don't try to beat me in a battle of dialectics, Sampedro. You've made a bad choice of prey. You should go after a jerk like General Pozzi, or Colonel Estevez. You could play with them until you're sick of them. But not with me. I read, I study. My war against you is not just about defending economic interests. It's a crusade, Sampedro, and you'll never beat me this way."

Sampedro watched his companions and gave them a gesture of approval. But the one who spoke was Zelinsky.

"Be careful what you wish for."

Iribarren speared Zelinsky with a look. "I hope to wake up and get this over with, that's what I hope, that you disappear from my horizon. I hope to cross this damned park and get home to my family, to eat dinner, to read a little before bed. Do you envy that? I have it, you lost it. I won. I won, dammit!"

Iribarren twisted his head from side to side; the crack of his spine was audible in the calm, warm night.

"No, Colonel," Sampedro said, "the game continues. And the prospects are good for us to force your position."

Iribarren, without warning, charged the first row of the dead, though he failed to surprise them. They moved aside, and Iribarren stumbled and fell inelegantly into the undergrowth. Laughter echoed and then died out.

"Don't try to prove that we're ghosts," Zelinsky said. "That's not the question, Iribarren."

Iribarren got up with dignity, and started toward his house without a backward glance. He told himself that nothing remained behind him but a few threadbare wisps of delirium, and that he would not give those low-life dead people the pleasure of seeing him look back.

The closer Iribarren got to his house, the more insubstantial it all seemed. He knew that a little normalcy, finding everything in its familiar place, would sweep away the last vestiges of the hallucination. It had to have been a hallucination.

He knew what waited for him, and the knowledge tucked around him like a cloak. He recalled each detail with precision, and the inventory gave him psychic strength. The garden, the dog, the grill where he cooked his sausages and steaks, the orange tree, his gun cabinet—they all brought him back to reality. He was sure now that it had been a nightmare, or the ill effects of something that he'd now shaken off.

He thought of Lucia, maybe a little irritated by the delay, going back to warming the food; of Martita, rubbing her eyes, stubbornly resisting the tidal waves of sleep; and of Gonzalo, impatient but disciplined, obedient to his father's command that he not go out without exchanging a few words. Strong habits are hard to break, they said.

A single shiver went through him from head to foot when the house came into view. The lights were out, as if there were nobody home. It was deeply wrong, somehow. Between his previous life and the eternal and superior life that would surely follow, there had been nothing but fundamental, foreseeable events; he had worked hard to make it that way.

He blinked, and the lights came on—with a flash, like the ones in the park. Was there an incompetent cameraman moving in the shadows of the willows, a clumsy pawn who was distracted by the slightest thing and forgot to put the necessary elements in the scene?

Iribarren recovered and walked the last few meters to the front gate. The barking of Bismark, his Dalmation, who had caught his scent from afar, closed the circle of invisible signs. He let the dog jump on him like a brazen acrobat as he opened the gate, then finally pushed him aside with a slap of the hand. He slid the key into the lock of the massive wooden door and, unable to contain himself, cried out, "Lucia, I'm home!"

In response he heard a strange kind of silence, composed of minute particles of noise. Noises that folded into themselves, noises of toys rolling over a pile of sand, noises tossed across a room by a clumsy hand, odd, obtuse noises. The noise that actors made, he suddenly realized, changing costumes between one act and the next.

He sensed the whisper of dull and murky thoughts, and their names knotted up in his throat. Lucia, Martita, Gonzalo. He wanted to speak them aloud and couldn't.

"Here I am," said a gruff voice. The shadows of the kitchen spat out a woman. She was drying her hands, dragging her feet, snorting. She was Rosa Naranjo.

"What are you doing in my house?" said Iribarren, or almost said it, because the words dried up in his mouth. But the woman knew how to interpret his grunt.

"What am I doing in my house? Cooking for the señor, who'll be home any minute."

"Where's Lucia?"

"Who's Lucia?"

"The children, where are they?"

"Here I am," said the child that Rosa had held by the hand in the park. Iribarren looked at the child for the first time. She was dark, with bulging eyes, and she looking nothing at all like Martita. But she wouldn't leave him in peace. "Marcelo won't let me play with his toys."

Marcelo. Toys. It wasn't possible. How could this have happened? Where was his real family? Lucia. Martita. Gonzalo.

"Your father's here," the woman said to Iribarren. "With no warning, as usual."

"My father?" Iribarren turned to look at the walls, not understanding how his father could be part of the conspiracy.

"He's in the den, playing chess with Marcelo."

Iribirren had had enough. It was time to skip the maneuvering. He threw himself against the door to the den, and the force of it knocked over the chessboard and chessmen. It was Zelinsky and Metralla.

"What are you so nervous about?" said the old man. "Something wrong?"

"Wrong?" Iribarraen stared dumbfounded at the four knights, which by chance had landed together on the white rug. "You sons of bitches! Trash!"

"Jorge, what's going on with you?" said Zelinsky. "You're scaring me. Marcelo, your father is—"

"Crazy?" Marcelo shook his head. "He's not crazy. He's just a little upset by something that happened in the park. Isn't that right, Papa?"

"Nothing happened to me in the park. What could have happened?" Iribarren suddenly snapped his hands out like whips, and was shocked when his fingers touched the old man's throat and managed to close around it in a steel grip. Outside, Bismark barked.

"What...are you doing?" stammered the old man. Marcelo pulled Iribarren's arms apart easily; all the confusion had sapped Iribarren's will. The solidity of the old man's flesh. The texture of the vertebrae, the prickly hair at the nape of his neck. The freezing tentacle of a nightmare that had gone on too long.

"What did you do with them?" Iribarren said.

"With who?" Marcelo said calmly. He was a few years older than Gonzalo, fatter, and cold. It would not have taken much for him to kill Iribarren's son.

"Are we going to eat tonight or what?" came the coarse voice of Rosa Naranjo. "The baby is dying of hunger."

"You don't exist," Iribarren said again. But once the words were out, he lowered his arms, defeated.

"Okay," he said. "You win. You want me to say it? Okay, I'll say it. I'm a bastard, a killer. I humbly beg your pardon for everything I've done, for what I made you suffer, and for having killed you. Is that enough? Now give me back my family."

He knew he didn't sound credible, but he was out of ideas. His guns were out of reach, and he was sure they wouldn't do any good. It was too late for any of that.

The imposters, the substitutes, the frauds, the fakes, moved as if they had learned to dance in an elevator, with tight little steps.

"So we don't exist?" Zelinsky said. "How much more proof do you need before you accept reality—the reality that is not what you want it to be? Family? We are your family, your only possible family. You'll learn to live with us, don't worry."

"You're not real," Iribarren sobbed. "I killed you. I killed Bernal with a full clip. All of you. Do you need me to put it in writing? Do you want me to go to the newspapers, the TV networks? Fine, I will. What more can I do?"

"Again with the show of guilt?" Rosa waved her hand in annoyance. "Once a week now, soon every day."

"What's the matter with Papa, Mommy?" said the little girl, who was not Martita.

Iribarren raised his eyes and got some strength back. "Very clever. Very shrewd. So you are the only family that I deserve. I never thought you could be so ingenious."

"Are we ever going to eat?" Rosa asked, impatient.

"No, I'm not going to eat," Iribarren said. "I have things to do."

"Now what?"

"Carry on with your game, since you're having so much fun." Iribarren turned his back on them and left the room, left the house. Nobody tried to stop him from taking out the car, or got in his way as he drove to the barracks. It was late, he knew, but he had no other choice.

He drove like a man possessed. He drove though all the red lights and got there in ten minutes. His tires skidded on the gravel as he pulled up in front of the barracks. He left the engine running and the car door open. Taking the three steps in a single leap, he burst into General Pozzi's office gasping and shaking.

"What's wrong, Colonel? Are you sick?" Sampedro took a cigarette out of his jacket and lit it with the same hand, in a gesture that Iribarren found neither magical nor natural. He looked into the eyes of the man behind the desk, with his dark complexion and curly hair, his aviator's jacket, canvas pants, and leather boots, and knew that the circle had now completely closed, and there was no force in the universe strong enough to break it and set him free.

✗

THE CANTOR AND THE GHOST

by G. Miki Hayden

The cantor, Mordechai Samuelson, was called in to rid the Alexander apartment of its ghost. Why the cantor and not the rabbi? Because the rabbi was dead, and likely the one haunting the Alexanders—and because everyone trusted and relied on the cantor.

Though many in the small Brooklyn congregation had come to find Rabbi Wild a bit on the tactless side, none had been more critical than Saul Alexander, whose father had helped found this very synagogue. Alexander, a dentist, was perhaps hypersensitive to miniscule matters of tradition here, and needled the rabbi endlessly over every one of these.

In fact, though Rabbi Wild and the dentist had been at odds for the last 10 years, it had started (the way Samuelson understood the affair) as a matter of herring. Herring? Yes, herring, or really the issue of herring in cream sauce versus herring in vinegar.

The topic for the two men hadn't been one of theory only. Called to advise on a dinner for Rabbi Wild's 50th birthday at a nearby kosher restaurant, Mrs. Wild had suggested as an appetizer her husband's favorite—herring in cream sauce. This became herring in vinegar under the stern command of Dr. Alexander. Herring in vinegar, though certainly thought to be more healthful by the dentist (and allowing for a meat entrée as well) wasn't to the liking of the Wilds.

A bitter yet not fully stated dispute arose thereafter between the rabbi and the dentist, resulting in years of controversy over such heated concerns as extra guest tickets for the High Holy Days; whether the rabbi should be reimbursed for his trip to a rabbinical conclave in Safed; the recarpeting of the rabbi's office; the very fraught debate regarding replacing the old seating in the sanctuary with theatre chairs; and any argument that could conceivably arise within the ordinary course of synagogue business.

So, if the rabbi had to pick someone to trouble after death, his selection of the dentist was entirely logical.

All this came to mind now as the cantor considered the rather antiquated but not completely non-Jewish idea of a haunting. After all, Samuelson mused, wasn't that why Jews covered the mirrors in a house after a death—for fear the soul of the dead-one might snatch the soul of the living?

Of course Cantor Samuelson didn't really know very much about ghosts. He wasn't even sure he believed in them—probably not—but he did always try to be agreeable. Not so young any more, though still in fine voice resonating with what he believed to be a pure, spiritual quality, he nonetheless stepped lightly around the members—who, after all, paid his salary.

"What makes you think you and your family are being haunted, Saul?" Samuelson began. His tone, he felt, was both polite and businesslike. Sitting on the Alexander couch, he had folded his hands judiciously in front of his paunch.

"That mumser *would* choose to haunt me and mine," Alexander fussed, an obvious nonanswer.

Samuelson summoned his meager knowledge of apparitions. "I mean, what manifestations, Saul?" He tried to smile at the dentist without revealing the discolored teeth in the back of his mouth. Dentistry, he feared, would alter his exquisite singing style, possibly affect his clear enunciation of the prayers.

"Well, someone or something blew out the Shabbos candles this Friday night, the exact moment that the rabbi died as we heard it later. I was *very* surprised." Samuelson nodded as if this might be a telling point, though perhaps one of the children had left a window open and the candles had been struck down by an errant wind.

"All of them, in different rooms, all together," added Alexander. "Malicious of him, don't you think?"

The cantor pondered. Or an angry child's prank?

"Well, afterward, I smelled that vanilla cigar he used to smoke. But that's not all…The following evening I found every single pair of undershorts in my underwear drawer cut to ribbons. Not even buried in the grave, and the man immediately begins his spiteful behavior from the other side. Just like him though. What a disgrace."

Samuelson squinched his face against the onslaught of terrible accusations. He hated to disagree, but really, how could he validate such a complaint?

He stood at once. "I'll study the books over this one, Saul. Don't despair. I'll do my best."

Hustling to the door, Samuelson had only a single regret: Saul hadn't offered him a cup of tea even, or a taste of one of his wife's famous strudels.

Samuelson went home and made himself a glass of hot Visoztsky's tea, which he drank with a lump of sugar in his mouth. Indeed Samuelson had been married once, but was a long-time widower; his son, a cantor in not-so-far-away Pittsburgh, came to see him briefly once or twice a year—but the older cantor enjoyed his solitude.

Tea by his side, Samuelson looked up at his bookshelves holding hundreds of volumes of Jewish law and lore in English, Hebrew, and in Yiddish. Surely some few lines in one of these—*The Shulhan Arukh* with Moshe Isserles's commentaries, the earlier *Arba Turim* (the "Tur") of Jacob ben Asher, or Karo's *Beit Yosef*—had his answers plainly written out in black and white.

Samuelson grabbed down book after book and riffled through, but strangely, he could find nothing specially associated with unwanted ghosts. Then, abandoning the more deeply considered advice to the observant, he pulled out a few of his books of folk tales to see if he could locate a bisel fitting guidance. In the index of the first two, he found something of what he was looking for—references to dybbuks and to their exorcism.

Maybe that was as close as he could come, though the idea of such unholy mishegoss unsettled his stomach. Surely the rabbi hadn't been so much of a sinner that he would turn into the most dreadful kind of demon.

Needing to take a break before even considering a ritual to send the recently deceased rabbi on to the world to come (a place Samuelson had no fixed concept of), he hopped up to boil more water in the kitchen for another go at the still-useful teabag. The Visoztsky's was perhaps a small indulgence for a man who preferred to spend his money on the mitzvah of charity—but just once around would hardly gain sufficient benefit from an expensive tea.

Returning to his sitting room, Samuelson nearly dropped his glass. Posed in the cantor's very own reclining chair as if it were a personal throne sat the recently buried Rabbi Wild puffing on a lit cigar.

"Lord of Hosts, protect me from all evil spirits," cried out Samuelson.

The rabbi frowned and snubbed his cigar against the wooden side table by Samuelson's La-Z Boy. "You call your rabbi an evil spirit?" he demanded of the cantor.

Samuelson, trembling, with the ends of his fingers about to burn from the hot tea, sat on the leather couch, and set his glass on his wife's cherished, pistachio-hued Tabriz rug. He stared defiantly at the deceased. "You," he said, using the word as an accusation. "You broke the Sabbath. Even a dead man should have more respect."

The rabbi recoiled. "Who broke the Sabbath? I? Not I."

The cantor, having caught the rabbi in the act, nodded briskly. "You blew out the candles in the Alexander apartment—and then tore up Dr. Alexander's undershorts—on Shabbos, yet." He was about to launch into a worthy Talmudic dissection of whether a man without a physical body may or may not be considered to have performed work, when the rabbi answered.

"No, cantor, no—the candles went out merely as a result of my rapid appearance there—and I traveled to that shmendrick's place completely under my own steam. As for tearing up his undershorts, I waited until the end of Shabbos to mete out justice." The rabbi relaxed, then picked up the discarded cigar, which resurrected itself and began to burn for the dead man to puff on—a trick Samuelson found decidedly spooky.

Wild hadn't violated the Sabbath at least. But Samuelson felt he needed to chide the rabbi, nonetheless, as a matter of fulfilling his scriptural duties. "Cutting up the man's personal garments, rabbi…"

"I know, I know," answered the surprisingly solid-looking apparition. "But Saul Alexander is a murderer. The man poisoned me—the reason you see me before you today in such lousy shape."

Duly troubled by the departed rabbi's charge, the next morning Samuelson called the synagogue president, Joshua Lefkowitz, and was invited to come to the doctor's office at 12:30, exactly, when Joshua had 10 minutes free. Samuelson arrived on time, of course, and was left to cool his heels in the waiting room for 45 minutes.

God forbid he should have a terrible disease and be made to wait this long, whining in misery.

Finally, the cantor was ushered in to the doctor eating at his desk. Samuelson stared at Lefkowitz's sandwich, not so much in hunger, but wondering where he'd gotten such a nice-looking meal. Samuelson was a man who cooked for himself, and dinner would be an apple and a can of tuna. But that was neither here nor there. He had only 10 minutes to get his point across.

"I'm shocked and saddened by the passing of the rabbi," the cantor began.

Lefkowitz gave him a quizzical look.

"Yes," said Samuelson. "He wasn't an old man. So tell me, precisely, of what did he die?"

The surprise on the doctor's face didn't diminish. "He had a heart attack and died well before the EMTs or I arrived."

"Maybe he was poisoned," suggested Samuelson. His own heart beat a little faster at the words. He knew how odd such a theory must sound—he embarrassed himself. And yet… "He insists that's what happened," Samuelson blurted out.

"Who insists?" asked the doctor. His expression had turned grave, with maybe the slightest undertone of anger.

The cantor could hardly admit where he'd heard the story—from the dead man himself. "One of the members," he mumbled in response. "I can't say who…but he believes strongly…strongly… that the rabbi was poisoned."

Lefkowitz continued eating his sandwich. Brisket maybe, with a slice of unusually well-ripened and juicy-red tomato. Perhaps Samuelson should try take-out a little more often, himself.

"I can assure you that all the signs were of death from a massive heart attack. Nothing at the scene—Nothing—Suggested anything else. Unless the unnamed member wants to accuse Edith Wild of poisoning her husband. He was home at least an hour after the service, showing no symptoms of any illness." Lefkowitz chewed, chewed, chewed, and swallowed, all the while gazing—or perhaps it might be called glaring—at Cantor Samuelson.

Even if Alexander *had* poisoned the rabbi, what was the cantor supposed to do? Exhumation was out of the question, expressly forbidden, unless they wanted to rebury the body in Israel.

Samuelson nodded. "A terrible loss," he said and stood. "I'm guessing the member who suggested poison was just upset. But I felt it my duty…"

"I had no idea," said Lefkowitz, "that you and the rabbi were so close. I was under the impression you two didn't get along."

Samuelson felt he got along with everybody. Sure the rabbi had treated him dismissively, as if the cantor was a mere side-dish to the main, rabbi-driven, course of the congregants's worship—but Samuelson followed the commandments, the mitzvot, telling him to love other Jews and not to bear a grudge. He was now quite upset with himself that he'd given the impression of disliking the rabbi. Well, no, upset with himself because he, in fact, had failed to love the unmannerly noodnik.

The cantor used his key to let himself into the synagogue, where he went and sat in the pigeon-hole office allotted him. He led perhaps a small and simple life, but why should he, a man whom Hashem had given such a large voice, care about that?

The cat who lived in the basement, Moses, walked in, tail up as if he owned the place, though only the week before the rabbi had been about to throw the poor thing out in the street, into the cold.

Now Moses demanded that his friend Samuelson acknowledge what a remarkable animal he was. The cantor took a moment to pet the cat. If anyone knew what went on in the synagogue, it was Moses. And half of what Moses knew, he'd learned from Samuelson, who told him everything. The rest of the fine points of the daily goings-on he probably got from seeing personally, with his bright emerald eyes.

"Moses, I can tell you because you're a smart cat and won't think I'm nuts, but I was talking to the rabbi the other day. Yes, his ghost. Imagine that. He said that Saul Alexander poisoned him. What do you think?"

Moses didn't answer immediately, so the cantor appealed to the Holy One and asked for a clue. *Did Alexander poison the rabbi? Or was the rabbi only blowing smoke?*

At just that second, Moses turned his back and walked away. Then the cat glanced around to make sure the cantor was following him, which, of course, looking for an answer to his heartfelt questions, Samuelson did.

Moses led his friend directly to the synagogue kitchen. Very interesting. The rabbi said Alexander had probably poisoned the coffee, so the place where Moses led Samuelson made perfect sense.

The coffee would have been thrown out days before and the pot washed by Izzy, the janitor. But the location indicated that the rabbi's allegation might be true.

After washing his hands, Samuelson opened the refrigerator to see if anything worth eating had been left behind by one of the members. He sniffed a plate of somewhat dried-out looking chicken. Not very appealing, but he gave a piece to Moses, who was happy to quickly devour his prize. Such a tidy creature, too, for he wet his paw and washed his face afterward. This was, indeed, a good Jewish cat.

Samuelson gave the cat a dish of water.

Turning around, he was startled to find the rabbi right behind him.

"Now that I think of it," said the rabbi, "maybe the chicken carried the poison."

Samuelson felt as if he himself had been fed a bitter pill. He openly wept. Had he killed an innocent animal—his best friend—Moses? He urged the cat to drink a little more water. Maybe they had an emetic in the first-aid kit? But where was it? Of course he could stick his finger past the animal's sharp teeth to make him disgorge what he'd thought was a treat, but the cantor feared he could hurt his good friend worse than even a poison.

In the end, Samuelson simply picked up the cat and carried him into the rabbi's office, where he closed the door and lay on the couch, not wanting the animal to live his last hour all alone.

His dear friend Moses had harmed no one—not a rude word in all these years—not a bite, not a swat, and Samuelson was well aware that the cat had plenty to grumble about.

The cantor fell asleep and woke to the sight of Joshua Lefkowitz standing in the doorway, staring at him. Was Moses still alive? Yes—and he jumped down from Samuelson's chest to go about the remainder of his daily routine.

Samuelson took a peek at his watch. He'd had quite a nap. Surely the chicken hadn't been tampered with.

"I *really* had no idea you were so devoted to the rabbi," Lefkowitz said.

Later that evening, Samuelson found Alexander at the shul, sitting in the sanctuary. Had the dentist something to feel guilty about? The cantor waited, then invited the dentist into his office for a glass of tea. He brought in the coffeepot full of hot water and looked to see if Alexander startled. Not a flicker of an eyelash.

Moses came in. He probably wanted to get the story firsthand.

"The rabbi said he had been poisoned," Samuelson stated, watching for the dentist's reaction.

Alexander stared, then blinked twice, apparently taking in the news that the cantor had been in contact with the rabbi.

"Oy. That would be terrible. No one could blame his soul for being restless if such a thing was true," said Alexander at once. "But who in the world would commit a deadly deed like that? Not a good Jew."

Moses rubbed against Alexander's pants' leg, while Samuelson popped a lump of sugar in his mouth, hoping the dentist wouldn't scold him for it.

But back to this thorny problem of a murder. Perhaps the suspect simply hadn't been goaded enough. "The rabbi thinks the poisoner was you."

Alexander set down his cup of tea before taking even a single sip. "And you would believe such a thing?"

"No, of course not. I'm merely reporting to you the facts."

Alexander seemed more annoyed than frightened. "I'm a family man," he said as if that were a sufficient alibi. "And if the rabbi himself said he was poisoned, he probably wasn't. That complainer."

Samuelson went to pay a condolence call on the widow, the rebbetzin, at an agreed-upon time—to speak to her privately. As anyone might logically expect, he opened with a few well-chosen words of sorrow, though he skipped the more usual expression of consolation. He couldn't be sure how Rabbi Wild had treated his wife at home, or how she felt about his passing. Indeed, in public she seemed devoted, but who knew what went on within her mind and heart? In fact, maybe the rebbetzin *had* poisoned the rabbi.

She asked Samuelson into the rabbi's den and offered him a glass of schnapps, which she brought forth momentarily with a service of tea and a plate of hamentaschen. He praised the poppy-seed pastry mightily while she giggled like a schoolgirl.

Then, though with a respectful sense of caution, he got down to business. "Is it possible, perhaps, and I'm only saying I heard someone mention, and it's just a silly thought, but could the rabbi have been poisoned?" He closed his mouth in order to concentrate on the woman's reaction.

"Oh, for goodness sake," Edith Wild retorted. "He came to you and gave you that ridiculous fairytale? Who in the world would poison that man? He told you Alexander, right?"

She looked at him, expecting an answer, but Samuelson was stunned into an immediate silence. Had who told him what? Were they talking about her husband, who, of course, was dead? How could she know the cantor had seen the rabbi's ghost? He felt he needed to lie down for a minute to recover.

Her mouth broadened as if for a 'tsk tsk.' "The rabbi," she said impatiently. "My husband. He's going around all upset saying that the dentist Alexander poisoned him." She shook her head. "Have another hamentaschen, my dear cantor. You're losing weight without a wife to cook for you. That man…" Her hands rose into the air. "This is so typical of my late husband, cantor, to blame someone else for what he's done. He ate too much. He smoked too much. We had to live practically inside the shul so he wouldn't have to walk too far and get a little exercise. I told him time and time again—'go to the doctor.' But would he listen? No. Of course not. So he drops dead of a heart attack, and blames—who else? The dentist, of course. Oy, vey is mir."

"I also had a visit from the rabbi after his death," Samuelson admitted, taking a deep breath.

"Of course, you did. He knew you to be an honest man he could depend on," said the housewife. "He knew you would give his claim a fair hearing. So, well, now, cantor, what do you think?" As she spoke, she once again offered Samuelson the dish piled high with her mouth-watering pastries, and he couldn't help but take a third.

"I think he died of a heart attack as Lefkowitz diagnosed…" Samuelson answered. "But he has no son. Perhaps you'll let me recite Kaddish for him in a son's place." Saying Kaddish for a rabbi he wished he'd liked better would do him some good.

"That's very kind, cantor. You're very thoughtful." And the rebbetzin poured him another cup of tea and passed him the cream. "I hope you'll come and visit me once more in a couple of days since I intend to make some apricot hamentaschen. No, better yet, I'll cook you a nice red-pepper soup and leg of lamb with a potato kugel."

"I'll be sure to drop by again," Samuelson said. But he decided he wouldn't. She'd already killed one man with all her abundance—serving heavy cream no less for the tea. A person could only take so much. "And for now, what shall I tell the rabbi if he shows up again?"

"Oh, he won't come," said the rabbi's wife. "I told him to move on and go where's he's supposed to be. He usually listens to what I say." She smiled in triumph.

Samuelson, puzzled by the contradictory description of her husband's listening/not listening to her, said nothing in response.

Carrying a bag of fresh pastries the rabbi's wife had given him, the cantor went straight to Alexander to report the outcome. But when the dentist invited Samuelson to dinner, already sweating because his stomach was so full, the cantor declined.

And besides, like the dear departed Rabbi Wild, Cantor Samuelson was not such a fan of herring in vinegar.

✗

THE COMPOUND

by Marc Bilgrey

It started out as a job like many others I've had in Palm Beach, Aspen, or Santa Barbara. This one was in New England. To say the place was huge would be an understatement. The grounds of the compound (no one ever called it an estate) were as big as Central Park, and the buildings were the size of airline hangars. The amazing part is that most of the time I had the whole place to myself. As the resident caretaker, it was my job to make sure that everything ran smoothly. After my daily patrol of the grounds on a golf cart, checking the perimeter monitors, and the motion detectors, I was on my own. Once a month I'd take a car out of the garage and drive ten miles into the nearest town to pick up some groceries. The truth was I really didn't need to go off the property at all, as my employers, the Jensens, had a least a year's worth of food in their storage freezers, and enough of it to feed an army; it was just an excuse to get away and see other human beings. Having only relocated a few months earlier, I didn't know or speak to anyone in town.

Every so often there'd be a delivery to the compound, which I would sign for, or a landscaper to cut the grass or trim the hedges, but, for the most part I had total peace and quiet. I often went into the compound's library, pulled a book off a shelf, curled up on a soft sofa, and started reading. Sometimes I'd watch a TV show on one of the wall sized screens and surf more channels than I ever knew existed. Or I'd take a swim in the heated indoor Olympic-sized pool, or find something from the vast music archive and listen to it. Once in a while, the boss or his wife would call to check in. I didn't make any calls. When you move around as much as I have, it's hard to make friends.

Since my divorce, (she left me for another guy), I've been drifting through life, never staying in one place or one job for longer than a few months. But this was different. Since coming to work at the compound I'd had a lot of time to think, and had made a decision. I would stay, start saving my money, and with a little luck, in a few years, I'd have enough to open a small restaurant. Maybe someplace that would serve nouvelle cuisine or Asian fusion. I'd worked as a chef in enough bistros, pasta joints, and even diners to have the experience, and had my ex-wife not cleaned out our bank accounts when she left, I'd already have been well on my way. But now I had a plan. It felt good after five years to finally have some hope again.

It was a cold day in January, when Kira Jensen drove through the front gates and made her way along the mile of rutted road that led up to the house. I hadn't been expecting her, but since it was as much her place as her husband's she didn't need a formal announcement. I went out to her Volvo and helped her with her bags.

"How've you been, Tom?" she said, as she walked into the house.

"Fine, Ms. Jensen, and you?"

"Very well, thank you. How're things here?" she asked, taking off her woolen hat and letting her long blond hair cascade to her shoulders.

"Everything's quiet, as usual."

"Good," she replied, removing her ski jacket and going into the dining room.

I followed, waiting to find out if she needed anything. She walked over to the bar, opened a bottle of Jack Daniels, poured some into a glass, and took a long gulp. Then she looked up at me. Though she was at least ten years older than me, there was no denying her beauty. Her high cheekbones, full lips, and bright blue eyes bespoke her Viking ancestry. And then there was her tight sweater. But despite her obvious charms, I was only an employee, and wanted to stay one. The surest way to get fired was to cross that line.

"Drink?" said Mrs. Jensen, holding up a glass.

"Uh, no thanks."

She shrugged, sitting down on one of the leather Chesterfield couches. She gestured to a nearby chair, and I sat down.

"The traffic coming up from Boston was brutal. You'd think that after two days they'd have dug out all the snow. But no, now there's ice to deal with. I must've passed at least half a dozen accidents."

"Ice can be dangerous," I said.

She sighed. "John's going to be in Barbados for the next couple of months. Claims it's a banking matter."

John was her husband. I nodded. Sometimes part of the job is being a bartender, priest, and psychologist.

"I understand there are quite a few banks in Barbados."

"And quite a few women, too," she said, then stood up abruptly. "I'm sorry, I'm tired, I'm going to my room to rest."

She set her glass down on an end table, near an ornate lamp, and went to the foyer. When I walked over to try to help with her bags, she shooed me away, and disappeared into the recesses of the house.

I wondered what all that was about, then decided that it was none of my business, and walked into the kitchen and poured myself a glass of milk. After I drank it I went to my room. Later, as I lay in bed, I thought back to my early days on the job in the waning weeks of the summer, when Mrs. Jensen and her husband were staying at the compound. They'd seemed happy and carefree, as they took walks, swam, and had their meals together. I remember watching them and thinking that they looked like a couple you'd see in a TV commercial. They seemed to have it all: looks, wealth, and each other. And yet, I couldn't help noticing Mrs. Jensen's glances at me. At first I thought it was my imagination, then when I realized it wasn't, I started inventing things I had to do on remote parts of the property. When she and her husband left after labor day, I was relieved. And now she was back. Alone.

In the morning I made some scrambled eggs and toast for Mrs. Jensen. She invited me to join her, but I declined, blaming my chores. I didn't see her again till that afternoon. I was out by the lake, pulling some fallen tree branches out of the water, when I looked up. She was standing there, framed against the fading sun, resembling nothing less than Botticelli's Venus.

"The last man who worked here quit," she said, walking toward me. "He said he couldn't handle the loneliness."

"I don't mind it," I said, dropping the branches near some rocks, "it gives me a chance to think."

"What do you think about?"

"All kinds of things."

I took off my work gloves and we began walking back to the main building.

"I think a lot, too," she said.

"Sometimes I think too much," I said.

I tried to come up with an excuse to get away from her but nothing came to mind. When we reached the house she asked me if I could cook her something simple for dinner. She told me to surprise her. I went to one of the freezers near the kitchen, found some chicken, potatoes, celery, carrots, broccoli, zucchini, all grown on the property, then I walked into the kitchen, took down a stainless steel pot, and a cast iron wok, and got to work.

"This is fantastic," said Mrs. Jensen, a little later, as she sat at the oak dining table, digging into her stir fried chicken. "I insist that you sit down and join me for this excellent meal."

I reluctantly agreed, doled some food onto a plate, and sat down at the far end of the table.

"Where did you learn to cook like this?" She asked, sipping a glass of Chardonnay I'd selected from the wine cellar.

"I went to school," I said. "I was going to open a restaurant."

"What happened?"

"I got sidetracked."

"It's not too late. You're a wonderful cook."

"Maybe someday."

After dinner Mrs. Jensen had me light a fire in the fireplace. Afterward, I tried to exit gracefully, but she wouldn't have it.

"Don't go, Tom," she said, sitting on a chair near the fireplace.

It wouldn't hurt to keep her company, I thought. And as much as I hated to admit it, it was nice to have someone to talk to.

"Have you ever been married, Tom?"

"Once," I said, "a long time ago."

She looked at me, then at the flames. "Marriage isn't easy. John and I have been together for twenty five years. We have an arrangement. He has his life and I have mine. But it's understood that we always come back to each other."

I nodded. My face was flushed. I wanted to tell her to stop talking, or change the subject.

"This time it's different," she said, "he's really found someone. And if that isn't bad enough, she's almost as young as our daughter. I've been told by people in the know that he actually claims to love her. Can you imagine?"

I swallowed.

"A plaything is fair game, but when it gets serious, well, something has to be done," she said.

"Uh," I said, standing up, "I really don't know if you should be telling me all this."

"Why not?" she said, "You're intelligent, sensitive. I have the feeling that you understand what I'm going through."

"Look," I said, "Mrs. Jenson …"

"Kira."

"Kira, I don't think it's right what your husband has done, but he's my boss, and—"

"I'm your boss, too."

"Yes, of course, I wasn't suggesting—"

"I know you weren't."

"I just think that maybe this is a discussion for a close friend."

"You're a friend."

"I'm an employee."

She looked into my eyes and said, "I'm sorry. You're right, of course." She turned back to the fire, seemingly lost in thought.

I spent the next few days trying to stay as far away from Mrs. Jensen as I could. I got up extra early, cooked breakfast and left it for her, then went outside on my rounds. I returned for dinner, but after preparing it, I made up a variety of responsibilities that required my attention—mending a fence, checking on drainage pipes, anything to get away. She seemed to be keeping her distance, too. And she didn't once call my cell while I was roaming the grounds. As much as I tried to avoid it, I found myself thinking about her. Her sexy smile, her blue eyes, her intelligence and warmth. It felt good to be attracted to someone. It made me feel as if I was alive again. Not that I intended to act on my feelings, but just knowing that I could still experience anything other than loss and sadness was comforting.

One night, after taking a hike in the woods, I returned to the house and found Mrs. Jensen on the couch, near the fireplace.

"If I didn't know better, I'd think you were avoiding me," she said.

"W-why would I do that?" I said, taking off my coat and hat and placing them on a nearby chair.

"Sit down on the couch," she said, smiling, "I won't bite."

I'd run out of excuses, so I went to the far end of the couch and sat down. She was wearing a low cut white blouse better suited to July than January. Despite myself, I glanced down, then back up at her face. She smiled as I realized that she'd seen me checking her out.

"He's leaving me, you know," she said.

"Your husband? But how—?"

"I have my sources. There's no question about it."

I looked at her, uncertain of what to say.

"It's unusual in our set," she said, pushing some of her blond hair behind her right ear, "divorce. It's still frowned upon. Upsets the bloodline."

"Ruling class," I said.

Her eyes sparkled. "They don't call it that in this country. We like to pretend there's no class system. In many ways we're still very provincial here, but the old world has no such illusions." She picked up a wine glass from a nearby coffee table and took a sip, then looked at me. "You probably know that my people are very blunt."

"So I've noticed," I said.

"Anyway, the point is that I like you and I know that you like me."

"You're, uh, a likeable person."

"In a very short time my husband will be out of the picture, so we won't have to worry about him. Not that it was ever a consideration of mine. But I can see that it's something that's been on your mind."

"Do you have telepathy?" I asked, smiling.

"I'm a woman and you're not a very good actor," she said, taking another sip of her drink.

My heart was racing. I stood up, walked to the fireplace and looked at the dancing flames. I thought that if I stared hard enough I might receive some divine wisdom that would tell me what to do next. But that didn't happen. After a minute or two Mrs. Jensen came over and stood next to me. Together we watched the fire and didn't speak. As we walked back to the couch she grabbed me and kissed me hard on the lips. I put my arms around her and felt her breasts press against my chest. Then her tongue was in my mouth and we fell onto the couch. Not long after, we made our way to the master bedroom and the king size canopied bed. She was wild and insatiable. And maybe I was too. Five years of being alone will do that to a man. I fell asleep in her arms with her scent in my nostrils.

When I woke up, it was morning and she was gone. I got dressed and went out to look for her. I found her in the solarium, next to a potted palm. Staring through the glass walls, at the forest in the distance.

"Hi," I said.

"Hi," she said glancing at me, then back at the trees.

"Are you all right?"

"I'm fine," she said, with little conviction.

My first thought was that I'd been nothing more to her than a one night stand. Had I disappointed her? Or was she just bored with me?

"I made a business decision recently." she said, "I'm just thinking about it." Then she turned to me, and said, "Shave, take a shower. Then we'll eat something and take a walk."

When I went back to the kitchen Kira was at range with a frying pan. She slid an omelet onto a plate, handed it to me, and said: "You're not the only one who cooks around here."

"Let me guess," I said, "The Sorbonne?

She smiled.

After breakfast we put on our coats and walked through the woods. Winter light seeped through the tall evergreens, and cast long shadows on the cold ground. Kira hardly spoke and I could see that she was preoccupied. I'd had a good thing going and now it felt like everything had changed. I was at her whim. Not only could she end what she'd started, she could fire me without a second thought. I went to my room and pondered my foolishness. Had I said or done something wrong? After a while, I went out and took another walk.

I lost track of time, because when I got back it was early evening. I found Kira in the library sitting at the Chippendale desk. As I approached, I said, "I'm sorry, I haven't prepared dinner. What would you like?"

"I'm not hungry," she said, staring at the leather-bound books that lined the shelves.

"If you change your mind…"

She nodded and I left the room. A couple of hours later, I was sitting on my bed, listening to a Felix Mendelessohn piece on my clock radio, when I turned and saw Kira standing in the doorway.

"May I come in?"

"Of course," I replied, turning off the radio.

She sat down on one of the room's two chairs, near the table. After a minute or two, she said, "He's dead."

"Who?"

"John. My husband, John."

"What happened?"

"He had an accident in Barbados. Fell off his boat. Drowned."

"That's horrible," I got up and went over to her. "Is there anything I can do?"

"Just hold me."

We embraced for a long time. She was sobbing. Then she pulled away. "I'm going to my bedroom. I'd like to be alone."

"Of course," I said.

So that's what she'd been so preoccupied with all day: the death of her husband. I glanced at the radio. It was nine o'clock. It all seemed suddenly surreal, like a dream. First the night before, now this. What a tragedy. And yet, I couldn't help wondering how this news would affect us. If, in fact, there was an 'us'. A divorce is one thing, a death was another matter. It was so overwhelming. And Kira was obviously in shock. They'd been together a long time. I'd have to step back, give her room to breathe. I felt very out of sorts when I got back into bed again. A day ago I knew what to expect out of life, now it seemed like all bets were off. My sleep was troubled, filled with dark dreams.

The next morning I got up, took a shower, shaved, and got dressed. Instead of leaving my room, I sat at the table, dreading what might be waiting for me. There was a lot to do right now. Arrangements to be made, people, no doubt, to be called. It seemed overwhelming. I didn't want to do anything, or talk to anyone. I didn't want to leave my room. I turned on the radio. The weather report came on: "—once again, the temperature is twenty five, going down to fifteen…and now back to one of the stories we've been following, the death of industrialist John Jensen. At one o'clock this morning, Jensen was reported missing by crew members of his yacht, near Bridgetown, Barbados. After an extensive search of the area by local authorities, his body was recovered at eleven this morning. The boat's crew were questioned and then released. Island police are calling it an accidental drowning."

I shut off the radio, and slumped in my chair. As I was staring at the wall, there was a knock on my door. When I didn't respond, Kira opened the door and stepped inside. She was wearing a long black dress.

"You look awful," she said.

"I'm sorry," I said. "How are you ?"

She gave me a half smile. "I'm holding up," she replied. "I have a lot of things to attend to."

"Of course," I said.

She left the room. I waited a few minutes, then put on my coat and took the back way out. I found myself at the lake, with so many thoughts in my head, it felt like it might explode. The timeline was all wrong, of course. Kira had been moody the whole of yesterday, and that was before she'd told me the news at ten PM. Even then it was four hours before her husband had been reported missing, and ten hours before the body was found. And that's not even considering the fact that Barbados is one hour ahead of Eastern Standard Time. The question was: what should I do? Call the police? Or ignore the whole thing and go on as if nothing had happened. I looked at the lake and thought about how it felt being with her the night before last.

"That little radio of yours is very loud," said a voice. I turned and saw her standing near me. "I was in the hallway."

For a moment she stared at the lake, then said, "No one will believe you."

"Why is that?" I asked.

"Because you are a servant," she replied.

The word stung. "I'm sure the police—"

"We own this town," she said.

"Then the next one…" I said.

"Who do you think put our state's two senators in office?" she said, then looked away. "Whatever did or didn't happen fifteen hundred miles away doesn't concern you. Why don't you just forget about it?"

"I…I don't know what to do."

"You seemed to know exactly what to do the other night," she said, smiling.

She looked at the water again, then said, "John and I had been together for a lifetime. I'm sorry it happened."

"You make it sound like it was meant to be."

"Some things are inevitable. It was all scheduled to take place a few hours earlier, but there was a delay, which I didn't find out about until later, as you noticed. Hence my confusion about the time. Oh, well, it was an honest mistake."

I felt a chill go down my back. Then she looked at me and said, "I've been thinking about your future. "How'd you like to have that restaurant you talked about?"

"What do you mean?"

"I'm a businesswoman, I'd like to invest in you. You pick a location anywhere in the world, and I'll back you."

"Just like that?"

"Give it some thought," she said. With that she turned and walked off. I stood alone for some time, in a daze. A loud honking noise snapped me out of it. I looked up, and saw a flock of Canadian geese, flying across the overcast sky.

Dinner was a somber experience, punctuated by ringing phones, which Kira didn't answer. Afterward, I went outside, and began walking. I mulled over all that had happened, replaying Kira's words again and again. There was no arguing that there was a deep connection between us, much more than just the physical. She was romantic, passionate, and smart. I'd been attracted to her the moment we'd met. It could be an ideal life, filled with intellectual pursuits and luxury. An entree into another world, as different from the one I'd been living in as a barren wasteland is from a lush tropical paradise.

The woods on the property's north end bordered on a state forest. I went through the dense foliage slowly, so as not to get caught in the snare of the sharp brambles that seemed to grow everywhere. After a couple of hours, I found myself on a narrow dirt road. From there, I made my way to a paved two-lane highway, where I walked for another half hour. A few cars went by, and then I saw a truck approaching. I turned and stuck out my thumb. To my amazement, the truck pulled over and opened its passenger side door. A man with a baseball cap and a pock-marked face looked down at me and said, "Where you headed to?"

"I'm not sure," I said, "how about you?"

"Portland."

"Sounds good," I said, climbing inside and closing the door.

"Kinda chilly tonight," he said, as he stepped on the gas pedal.

"Yeah," I said.

Just then my cell phone rang. I pulled it out of my jacket and stared at it. It continued to ring. I opened the window and threw the phone into the dark forest.

"That looked like an expensive one," said the driver.

"Not everything has a price tag," I said, as I looked out at the long empty road ahead.

THE ADVENTURE OF THE MISSING COUNTESS

by Jon Koons

It was a glorious spring day in the year 1889. The air was still brisk, but surprisingly fresh for the city, and the walks and lanes down which I trod were lined with fragrant and colourful rosebay willow and London Pride.

I awoke this morning fully with the intent of escorting my lovely wife, Mary, at her request, to the traveling circus that had made nearby Tunbridge Wells its temporary home, but those plans were laid aside, much to my wife's dismay, by an urgent communication from my friend and associate, Sherlock Holmes. As I walked the accustomed route to 221 Baker Street, I reflected on some of Holmes's past adventures which started out in this exact same manner. Upon arriving at my destination, Holmes greeted me warmly.

"Ah, Watson, so good of you to come."

"Come, Holmes," I replied, "I have rarely declined an opportunity to accompany you on one of your cases."

"Quite so, but since Mary Morstan made an honest man of you, yor availability has been somewhat more limited."

"One of the small disadvantages of married life, I'm afraid."

"A small disadvantage to be sure. Married life agrees with you, old boy."

"Not that I disagree, mind you, but what leads you to that conclusion, Holmes?"

"Elementary, my friend. You have, of late, been more ebullient than ever. Your apparel has been more carefully coordinated, the obvious influence of a woman's keen eye for fashion, and is better tended to, save for the small stain there on your vest... kippers, I would say... which indicates that you are being well fed. The fact that your ample stature has become even more so by eight or ten pounds would tend to support this conclusion. You are more precisely groomed, your shoes are finely polished and you appear more rested and less tense, an obvious benefit of the sort of companionship that you formerly lacked. Your occasional discourse regarding your wife is always favorable, and the very fact that you have been less available to join me lately clearly indicates that you are enjoying your current situation and reaping the benefits."

"Holmes, you never cease to amaze me."

"Nor I myself, old boy."

"So, what are we onto today?"

"Come, Watson. I'll tell you all I know in the cab."

In the carriage, Holmes explained what he knew of the case.

"Do you know the name Countess Virginia Thorgood Willoughby?"

"As a matter of fact I do. I read an account of Lady Willoughby recently in the society pages of *The Strand Magazine*. If memory serves, she's a widow who lives alone with her seventeen year old daughter. She lost her husband during a visit to America last year, although the particulars of the event elude me."

"Very good, Watson. What else do you recall?"

"She returned with her daughter to London six months ago to leave the incident behind and raise her daughter with a sense of proper British morality, something which, according to the article, she found lacking in America."

"Precisely. She did not wish her young, impressionable daughter, Lady Alexandra, to succumb to the improper influences that she said the Americans seemed to thrive on. Apparently she was a bit too late, as her daughter was already enamored of American ways and was, by all accounts, unhappy with the sudden move back to England. She caused her mother a good deal of embarrassment by making her feelings known at every opportunity, not least of all in public."

"But what does this have to do with us?"

"It seems, Watson old man, that upon arriving home from the opera late last night, Lady Willoughby found her home a shambles and her daughter missing. She has not been seen since approximately five hours before the discovery of the transgression, which is why our destination is their Kensington residence. Lady Willoughby immediately sent word to Scotland Yard, who investigated with their usual fervor but aside from finding a concise ransom note, were unable to fathom the meaning of any of the available clues. As has happened more than once, as well you know, Inspector Lestrade sent for my aid, which he will gladly employ and thereafter forget to acknowledge. But no matter, my dear Watson. I have been hungry for a new mystery to occupy my time. I was, of course, dismayed to be called so long after the crime had been discovered, but Lestrade assures me that the scene, and any evidence which might be present, will be left undisturbed until our arrival. So now you know as much as I about this case, save that we are presently going to meet the Countess in the company of her legal advisor and recent social companion, Kent Osgood, whose role in these proceedings has yet to be determined."

"Surely, Holmes, this is a simple case of kidnapping, not worthy of your extraordinary talents."

"Perhaps, Watson," Holmes replied. "Perhaps."

Holmes then fell silent and gazed out the window, his fingers pressed together in a steepled attitude, as was his custom during moments of deep thought. As I looked upon my friend, bedecked in his customary deerstalker cap, cape-backed overcoat and pipe, all of which had become, I daresay largely due to my accounts of his adventures, his trade marks, I pondered my own good fortune not only to be in the presence of greatness, but to be his personal friend and longtime companion as well.

We arrived at the address in Kensington shortly afterwards and were ushered into the house with all due haste by a maid who appeared utterly distraught. She took us directly to the sitting room where Inspector Lestrade, the Countess and Mr Osgood were waiting. At once we could see the disarray caused by the perpetrators. Furniture had been knocked askew or overturned. Drawers were opened and rummaged through, and all manner of things were strewn about the room.

"Mr Holmes," cried the Countess, "I am at my wits' end. You are the only man in all of London that can save my little girl. Please say that you will help me."

"I shall do what I can, Lady Willoughby. Please try to calm yourself so that you may answer some questions for me."

"I will do my best," said the Countess as she grasped the hand of her companion. After some brief introductions, Holmes began his questioning.

"Lady Willoughby, I am told you discovered your daughter missing when you returned from the opera last night…"

"Yes, Mr Holmes, that is so. I blame myself. Had I not been out of the house last night for so frivolous a reason perhaps my little girl would still be here with me now…" She began to weep, and Mr Osgood embraced her.

"Now we've been all through that, Virginia. You are not to blame," said Osgood in a comforting tone.

"Mr Osgood is quite right. You cannot be held accountable for actions about which you had no prior knowledge. If I may continue? Is it your custom to frequent the opera, or was last evening a special event?"

"If I may, Mr Holmes," Osgood interjected. "Since Lady Willoughby and I have been keeping company these last several months we have made it a weekly ritual to visit the opera, or perhaps a concert. We generally do so on a Friday evening, but this past Friday Lady Willoughby was feeling a bit under the weather, so we postponed our weekly entertainment until last night, Tuesday."

"Was anyone else aware of this change of plans?"

"Not to my knowledge. It was the maid's day off. We had invited Alexandra, as we usually do, but she unfortunately declined, as she usually does."

"And at exactly what time did you leave the premises?"

"The opera we saw was *The Magic Flute*, at the Royal Albert Hall, which was to begin at eight o'clock. As you are no doubt aware, Albert Hall is not far, so we left here at a quarter past seven, I would say."

"And you returned…?"

"They returned," piped Lestrade, obviously feeling left out, "at exactly seventeen past midnight, according to my report."

"Thank you, Inspector. Your assistance, as always, has been invaluable. Now if you will permit me to inspect the premises I shall see what clues I can unearth. If you please, Watson."

As we began to scrutinise the room, Inspector Lestrade commented on the lack of available clues, save a knife thrust through a photograph of Alexandra hanging over the mantle. Holmes nodded. I followed my friend to and fro, carefully noting every item that he examined.

I spotted something unusual on the floor near the entrance.

"What do you make of this, Holmes?" I called out. He joined me at the door, stooped and pulled his glass from his pocket.

"Good show, Watson. Sawdust!"

"Sawdust? Then perhaps we are looking for someone in the construction trade. Or perhaps woodworking."

"Perhaps, Watson. Come look at this photograph. Young Lady Alexandria is quite an attractive lass, is she not?" She was indeed, I agreed. The hand-tinted photograph showed her long golden hair and lovely, delicate features.

Holmes pulled the knife from the photograph and handed it to me. "What can you tell me about this knife?"

"Well…" I studied the knife carefully but could not see what he was getting at. "The handle is worn more on the left side than the right, so…our suspect is left handed?"

"Excellent. Please continue."

"The blade is very dull, which means that it is used by someone who is either neglectful of its poor condition or else who does not require a sharp edge."

"Bravo, Watson. Very astute. There is more, but time is fleeting. Inspector," Holmes said, turning to Lestrade, "I would like to see the ransom note, then I want to inspect the girl's bed chamber."

"Here's the note. No point looking into the bedroom."

"Quite," was all Holmes said. He glanced briefly at the note and then handed it to me. "Please read this aloud, Watson."

"If you ever want to see Alexandra alive again, deliver a sum of one thousand British pounds to the Charing Cross train station on April 29th at noon. Put it in a small bag and leave it at the signal flag at track 9. Go to ticket window five afterwards and Alexandra will be waiting. Come alone. If we see police, I will kill her." As I finished reading, the Countess once again burst into tears.

Holmes asked the maid to direct him to the girl's bedroom, and went off directly, only to return a few moments later.

"I told you it was pointless, Holmes." Inspector Lestrade looked at me with a smug look.

"I have seen all I need to," Holmes replied simply. "I shall contact Watson three days hence and he shall relay my instructions. In the mean time feel free to tidy up the damage and go about your business. Lady Willoughby, your daughter is safe so you needn't fear. Three days, then!" And with that he nodded to the group and was out the door. Both Lestrade and Lady Willoughby were obviously bewildered, and looked to me for clarification, which I cold not provide.

I quickly followed. "No time to explain, Watson," Holmes stated, as he hailed a cab. "Be at Baker Street in three days." As he climbed into the cab, he turned and said, "And bring your lovely wife Mary with you."

"Holmes…?"

"Time is short, Watson. I've clues and motives to juggle." The cab started off.

Puzzled by Holmes' behavior. I took advantage of my proximity to Kensington Gardens, and strolled through the park pondering the events of the day. Could Holmes have pieced together the clues and unravelled the mystery so quickly? I had, of course, witnessed his uncanny abilities on numerous occasions before, but it seemed he reached some conclusion in an impossibly brief amount of time. Why did he leave so abruptly? What purpose would his three day absence serve? And to what end was my wife's presence requested? Think as I might, I could not decipher his reasoning. Winded from my exertions, I sat upon the steps of the Albert Memorial and watched two badgers frolic through some oxeye daisies, Mary's favorite flower. I knew only one thing for certain. Holmes had been right. I was putting on weight.

Three days later my wife and I arrived at Baker Street. It had been some little time since Mary had been there, but she remembered it well and felt quite comfortable, although no less curious than I about the circumstances. Shortly after our arrival, Mrs Hudson, the landlady, handed me a wire from Holmes. It instructed me, and Mary, to meet him at, of all places, R.J. Toby Colossal Travelling Circus in Tunbridge Wells. He entreated us to enjoy the three o'clock show, and then wait afterwards at the Torture King tent where he would meet us. Mary was delighted to be included in Holmes' adventure, but even more now that it appeared she would get to see the circus after all. We departed immediately for Tunbridge Wells.

The festival was a splendid sight to behold. A great tent, striped in bright red and blue, was the centrepiece to a dizzying display of colour and movement. Wonderful carriages, arranged in a half circle, resplendent in their brilliant reds and whites, were trimmed out with yellows and greens and gaudy rococo gold leaf. Some of the carriages bore cages which held magnificent beasts of all types, while others displayed performers' names and promises of wonders to come. While looking closely at a caged lion I discovered, curiously enough, that my inclination to sneeze while in the presence of common house cats was also very much a reality in the presence of these larger, rather less amiable cats, a fact which did not please me but apparently amused my wife no end. A carousel hosting painted horses and carriages turned round and round for the amusement of the children, and the sound of calliope music filled the air. Aromas of all types, some pleasant and some not so, assaulted the nose. The fair was quite a sight, sporting tall impressively illustrated banners describing the likes of such oddities as the Incredible Bearded Woman, the Tantalizing Egyptian Snake Charmer, the Amazing Dog-Faced Boy, and the Death Defying Torture King. I noted the location of the latter's tent for future reference. In our wanderings I saw no sign of Holmes. Having strolled the grounds of the circus, and after having partaken, at Mary's behest, of some sort of gooey confection made from nuts, bits of dried fruit, chocolate and caramel, much of which I was still trying unobtrusively to pry from my teeth, we headed for the main tent, as it was nearly three. While purchasing our tickets we were met by Lady Willoughby, Mr Osgood and Inspector Lestrade. I introduced my wife to the gathering, and we took seats near the large wooden ring which served as the stage area. The ring was floored with a generous amount of sawdust, and much to my dismay, I began to sneeze once again.

"Mr Watson..." began the Countess.

"Doctor, my Lady," I corrected her.

"Forgive me. Doctor Watson, I do not understand what we are doing here. Perhaps you can shed some light?"

"I should be delighted to, but I am as much in the dark as you. Sherlock Holmes is the most knowledgeable person I know, but I must confess that I still do not entirely understand all of his methodology. If it is any comfort to you, from what I know of my friend, you shall have your answers, and most likely your daughter, before the day is up."

Lestrade complained, "No good will come of building Lady Willoughby's hopes up. Scotland Yard has been investigating this case for three days as well, and we have drawn no conclusions. Holmes is good, I'll grant you, but I dare say he's not so good as to deliver Lady Willoughby's daughter on a silver platter!"

Mr Osgood agreed. "Yes, Dr Watson. Suppose you are wrong. I should think that instilling false hope is something you would wish to avoid."

"Mr Osgood, Inspector Lestrade," said my wife, "I was once a client of Sherlock Holmes. I am confident that he will solve this mystery and return Lady Alexandria to you. If anyone can, he can."

"Thank you, my dear," replied the Countess. "You are very kind."

At that moment, the crowd fell silent. The show was about to begin. Mary took my hand and we settled down to enjoy the show. Neither of us had been to the circus since we were children. The ringmaster, in his jodhpurs, red frock coat and top hat, introduced the acts each and all, and the band played merrily as the performers took their places in the large circular stage area. A lovely young lady led six stallions of varied colours around the ring, and demonstrated her mastery of horsemanship. The tent fairly vibrated with applause. Next, a colourful clown on stilts juggled three lit torches. He tried to blow them out, one by one, but every time he transferred them from hand to hand they relit, one by one, much to Mary's delight. Finally dousing the flames, he walked across the ring, but seemingly unaware of the tight rope which blocked his passage, became entangled in it. His stilts shot out from under him, leaving him dangling from the rope. After many precarious antics he gained the top of the rope and proceeded to walk its length to a small platform. He bowed to the thunderous applause of the crowd, and in doing so fell to the net below, and then ran off. Next came the elephants, followed by some acrobats and then it was again time for the clowns, this time several of them dressed in the costume of a fire brigade. The "fire clowns" ran circles around one another in an attempt to "save" a burning building, bumping into each other, falling down, dusting off, and falling down again. One clown jumped into the crowd, tweaked Mary's nose, pulled my moustache and bolted back into the ring. Mary told me that the clown was very familiar somehow, but I explained that he had been the same stilt-walking clown from earlier in the show. After the clowns had failed to "save" the building, they rapidly retreated from the tent, as the crowd roared with laughter. Several foreign chaps and scantily clad young ladies flew through the air on a tra- peze, after which a young man, about twentyish, I would say, led a teenaged boy to a door-sized wooden wall and fastened him to it by the arms and legs. The man then stepped back and displayed a set of dangerous looking knives, which he proceeded to throw directly at the boy. Mary held my hand as I caught my breath, and the crowd was silent with fear. He hurled the knives one by one, impaling them in the wooden wall, each time narrowly missing the boy. Only when the boy was completely surrounded by knives was he released and able to take his bows with the young man. Several additional acts followed, including trained dogs, more clown antics, a dancing Russian bear, and an additional display of acrobatics. At the end of the show, Mary and I, along with Lady Willoughby, Mr Osgood, and Inspector Lestrade, headed for the Torture King tent, which I took note of previously.

"How did you enjoy the show?" Mary asked the group as a whole.

"Very amusing," Lady Willoughby answered, although it was obvious she was distracted by other concerns. Osgood agreed.

"Well, since you asked," Lestrade said unpleasantly, "I think it was rubbish. All just stuff and nonsense."

We stood silently as a group in front of the designated meet- ing area, awaiting Holmes' arrival. Numerous patrons, and even many of the performers on their way to the changing tent passed by, but there was as yet no sign of Holmes. One clown, the featured performer throughout the show, stopped before us to further dis- play his antics. He pulled three coloured balls from a pocket and juggled them in a number of different patterns before tossing them high into the air and allowing them to fall directly on his head. His body crunched lower to the ground as each ball hit until he was flat on his back. Mary, Osgood, and I applauded. Lady Willoughby then turned to me and said,

"Dr Watson. While this is all quite amusing, I am finding it hard to keep my spirits light in the face of our purpose here."

"Quite right," added Osgood, "where is this Sherlock Holmes of yours?"

Just then the clown jumped up and onto his hands, where he stood momentarily. "I seem to have turned myself around. You all look so tall. But if I keep this up I'll lose my head." He righted himself, then placed a pipe between his teeth, from where he retrieved it I could not say, and then blew into the stem, causing a great cloud of ash to erupt into the air. "I say, would you have some tobacco that I can borrow? My pipe has gone empty."

"Well, no actually, I do not." I said.

"Just as well," said the clown, "it would probably smell like an old Persian slipper, anyway."

"As a matter of fact…wait a moment. How could you know that?"

"Elementary, my dear Watson."

"HOLMES!?"

"Holmes? Sherlock Holmes?" the startled Countess asked.

"What's all this then, Holmes?" Lestrade said.

"Excuse me, but I seem to be a bit confused…" Osgood said.

"All your questions will be answered. Please follow me." Holmes started off in the direction of the dressing tent and our party obligingly followed. "Sorry to have taken you all by surprise like this, but it was necessary," he explained. "My theatrical inclinations have been a long time without expression. It was good to utilize my talents once again." He stopped outside the tent, and proceeded with his explanation. "While at your home, Lady Willoughby, I found several clues which led me here. The sawdust on your floor was fouled with soil and animal refuse. Had it been tracked in from a carpentry shop or similar establishment it would have been purer." He removed his red rubber nose and yarn fringed bald pate wig. "The knife that impaled your daughter's photograph was not thrust in, but thrown from across the room, as indicated by the angle at which it hit. Furthermore, the knife is a specially balanced one, edged for use in a knife throwing act. The shattered glass from the frame was spread in a pattern that suggested an impact of great force. Had the knife been thrust into the photograph manually, the pattern would have been less remarkable. Finally I detected a faint odor of greasepaint in the room. Someone connected with this circus, the only one within reasonable distance, seemed the only logical choice."

"Astounding," I said.

"Simple deductive reasoning, Watson. The culprit, obviously an amateur, overturned and disturbed both furniture and belongings in an effort to simulate a robbery, or perhaps a struggle, but the ruse was unconvincing. Had he sought to rob the house, valuables would have been missing, and furniture left undisturbed. If the purpose of the break-in was a kidnapping, belongings would not have been touched, and had there been an actual struggle, I find it unlikely that large, heavy pieces of furniture would have been overturned while trying to apprehend a small, seventeen-year-old girl. "

"Mr Holmes," Lady Willoughby interposed, "you said at my house that my daughter is safe. How can you be so sure? And where is she?"

"She is here, my Lady. You have seen her. You all have."

"Here," objected Lestrade, "What do you mean?"

"You'll see soon enough. Please accompany me into the tent."

Once inside, we found ourselves in the company of several performers in varying stages of undress, many in the process of removing make-up. Holmes walked to the center of the room and spoke aloud. "Pardon me, but my friends have joined me so that we may solve a crime." He looked around the room, and his gaze fell upon the young man who had performed the knife throwing act, who suddenly appeared nervous, and began edging his way towards the exit. Holmes nodded to a burley toff, the Man of Steel, who blocked the young man's passage and said "Aye wouldn' go nowheres if aye was you," and so he gave up the attempt.

Now, young Master Errol Smithy, or should I use your real name, Chuck Hanson? I shall make a series of statements, and you will answer yes or no depending on the accuracy. You are personally acquainted with Lady Willoughby's daughter, Lady Alexandra, are you not?"

"Well, I…We kind of…" Hanson stammered and looked around the room for help, but none was forthcoming.

"Yes or no, Mr Hanson?"

"Yes."

"You are in love with Lady Alexandra, and have been since you met her in America last year."

"Hey, how could you know that?"

"That qualifies as a yes, wouldn't you say Watson?"

"Indubitably, Holmes."

"You have, in fact, been lovers, and plotted this kidnapping ruse so that you could be married."

Lady Willoughby gasped. Osgood helped her to a seat.

"Look, we knew her mother would never approve of us. I'm just a circus brat from the poor side of the tracks. We planned to get hitched back home in New Jersey, but when they moved back to England, I had to find a way to be with her. I sold all of my belongings, except my knives, and used all of my savings to book cheap passage to England and then got the job with the circus here. I contacted her as soon as I could and we planned the whole thing."

"Logically, your lack of money would present a problem, and hence the reason for the kidnapping ruse."

"At first we were just going to run off and elope, but I thought of the kidnapping scheme to get some money to make our start in life a little easier. Don't blame Alex. It's all my fault. I just love her so." He flopped down into the nearest chair and lay his head in his hands.

Holmes asked Lestrade for the ransom note. The inspector handed it to him. "This was the most incriminating piece of evidence in unravelling the puzzle. Attend. 'If you ever want to see Alexandra alive again, deliver a sum of one thousand British pounds to the Charing Cross train station on April 29th at noon.' The note refers to 'Alexandra', a familiar use of the name, indicating personal acquaintance. Secondly, the reference to 'British pounds' suggested to me that the "kidnapper" was someone who thinks in terms of a different monetary system. American dollars are unique and standard across that country, whereas the European designation of 'pound notes' as currency are issued by any of several countries.

Local residents would not specify the country of origin. Only an American in a foreign country would make such a distinction. Next point," Holmes continued. "The use of 'train station' rather than 'railway station' is American, as is the note's poor grammatical style in general. There are numerous other clues, but they are of no great moment." He handed the note back to Lestrade. "I left the home of Lady Willoughby and came immediately to this circus, where I was hired temporarily as a new performer. Over the past three days I have had the opportunity to discover, at leisure, all of the additional information that I required from the company of performers and from young Chuck himself. He is twenty one years old, from Hackensack, New Jersey, in America, and as you may have observed during his act, is left handed.

"When the circus arrived in Tunbridge Wells, the closest stop to London on the touring schedule, he and Lady Alexandra waited for an opportunity to carry out their plan. The only time Lady Willoughby left the house with any regularity was on Friday, but the circus had late performances those nights. When Lady Willoughby rescheduled her outing, it was exactly the turn of luck that they had hoped for. Tuesday is the only day on which the circus has no performances. It was a very fortunate happenstance indeed that the supposed abduction could be carried out without his absence from the circus being noticed."

"All right, Holmes." Lestrade interrupted, a little too loudly. "You've told us how you found him out, and that he had means and motive, but aside from what he says, what evidence do you have that the girl was involved of her own free will?"

"Inspector, your investigation of the Willoughby premises was incomplete. When I investigated Lady Alexandra's bed chamber, I took particular note of the items on, or rather the items missing from, her vanity and wardrobe. Nothing was disturbed to suggest a theft, but small gaps with empty hangers in the wardrobe indicated the removal of a few select pieces of necessary apparel. And no young lady of proper breeding would feel complete without her brush and hand mirror, which were conspicuously missing from the vanity. In addition, only Lady Alexandra knew the exact time that her mother and the maid would be away from the house, and for precisely how long."

"Mr Holmes, please. My daughter would never do such a thing!"

"I quite agree, Holmes." Osgood added. "Your conjectures are bordering on slanderous. I suggest you prove your theory immediately, if you can, otherwise I shall be forced to advise Lady Willoughby to file suit against you on behalf of her daughter."

"Kent, please!" The Countess chided. "I have no interest in proof or legal suits. I only want my daughter back. Mr Holmes, you have brought us all the way here to listen to your brilliant deductions, but where is my daughter?"

"Walking through that very tent flap at any moment." Holmes stated calmly. As if on cue, the tent flap pulled back and a lone figure entered the tent.

"Ha!" Lestrade scoffed. "It's just the boy from the knife act." The boy had entered, seeing a crowd of curious faces intently staring at him, and stopped frozen in his tracks. His face went ashen. Tears started to well up in his eyes.

"ALEXANDRA!" Lady Willoughby was beside herself.

"Hi, mummy," the girl said sheepishly through her tears.

"Lady Alexandra, indeed!" Holmes said triumphantly. "Hair dyed black and cut in the style of a young lad, dressed as a young lad, but Lady Alexandra, nonetheless. Her boyish figure made it a convincing disguise. I learned her habit to change costume out of sight of the others, but she always returns to the tent so as not to draw attention to her absence."

The Countess embraced her daughter.

"But why, Alexandra? Why?"

"Because I love him, mother."

"Well now," Lestrade coughed, embarrassed, "seems like Mr Holmes has done a right good piece of reasoning, after all. But it's all in the hands of the law now. I assume, my Lady, that you would like to press charges against this young scalawag?"

"No, Inspector, I would not."

"Virginia, really! As your legal advisor I must advise you to…"

"Do be quiet, Kent."

"Mother…?"

"I think we must all sit down and have a long chat," said Lady Willoughby. "If you love this boy so much that you staged this elaborate deception, and if he left behind his life in America to follow you here, well…we shall all discuss it at length when we get home."

"Oh, Mother," said the girl as she heartily embraced her dam. They walked out of the tent, followed by Hanson and Osgood, who, still cowed, nodded to us with a shrug before departing. Lestrade looked as if about to say something, but simply turned and left.

After the others departed, Sherlock Holmes took a seat and immediately began rubbing some sort of white cream on his face to remove the remains of his clown make-up. He spoke as he cleansed.

"Mrs Watson, so good of you to come."

"Likewise, Mr Holmes. But why did you ask me to accompany my husband?"

"Watson mentioned your desire to see the circus, which I so rudely interrupted. Besides, I wanted to see what it was that has been making my old friend appear so happy lately."

"Why thank you, Mr Holmes."

"Think nothing of it, Madame. Now then, you two must stay on with me for the next show."

"What on earth for?"

"I would like to see it rather than be a part of it just once…"

"Bye the way, Holmes," I asked, "how did you learn the juggling and stilt-walking and such?"

"Simply a matter of balance, coordination, and concentration, if one is physically fit. As a young lad I was always fascinated with clowns, so I learned the basics of the craft, thinking I might one day become a circus performer. It seems I've managed to do just that. I was able to learn the intricacies of the skills once I arrived. The routines themselves haven't changed much since I saw the circus as a boy, so I was familiar with them already. So, what do you say? Will you see the next show with me?"

"Mary and I would be delighted to spend an entertaining evening with my closest friend and companion. Can you, by any chance, deduce who that might be, Mr Sherlock Holmes?"

"I haven't a clue, Watson. I haven't a clue."

✗

THE HOME TOUR

by D. Lee Lott

We had been driving all day and finally arrived at the first house on the tour. I had purchased tickets for myself and my friend, Audrey, over the internet for a Celebrity Home Tour. Since we were both in the interior decorating business and partners of our own design firm (not to mention best friends), we were more than a little excited at the opportunity to see first-hand how some of the houses had been decorated. The tour group was to meet at the first house listed on the tour agenda and then a chartered bus would pick up the group there and take them on the remainder of the tour. We arrived a little earlier than we had anticipated and no one else from the tour group had gotten there yet, so we parked in the area that was designated for us and walked towards the first house. The tall wrought-iron gate was open, so we walked through into an immaculate front yard that sloped up towards the house. The walkway that led to the front door was broken up by small sets of cobblestone steps. It was simply, but nicely landscaped with delicate bushes all along the front of the house and a few scattered large elm trees in the yard with lush, dark green grass. The front door was also open, so we cautiously peeked in and called out to see if anyone was there. There was no response or any sounds, so we walked in. The house was as beautiful as one would expect a celebrity house to be, with rich shades of deep gold and beige. This one was a huge two-story with over 10,000 square feet.

We thought since no one was here yet, that it wouldn't be a problem if we changed our clothes and freshened up a bit after our long drive. We decided to use one of the bathrooms upstairs just to change in as long as we didn't disturb anything. I walked back to the car to get the small travel bag which contained a change of clothes for each of us, but still didn't see any signs of our tour group. As I walked back in the door, I saw Audrey at the top of the stairs so I started heading in her direction when I suddenly heard voices coming from the kitchen. At first I thought other people on the tour had arrived until I heard the voices become raised and angered. I suddenly felt panicky, like we shouldn't be there. I set down the bag and quickly caught up to Audrey and told her we needed to get out of there now. My intuition was strongly pushing me to leave and I heard footsteps behind us as we neared the front door. In my hurried state, I forgot to pick up the travel bag as we all but ran down the driveway towards the gate and street. As we were rushing down the driveway, we saw three cars that weren't there when we arrived and they were parked in such a way that they half blocked the long driveway to the house. They must have driven in right behind me as I was returning with the travel bag. We quickly walked past them, checking to see if there was anyone inside. When we got to our car, I told Audrey about leaving the bag and that we would have to come back to get it when we were comfortable that other people from the tour would be there. We decided to go ahead and check into our hotel room just to kill a little time. We planned on staying overnight, since the tour would take up the biggest part of the day and it was a three hour drive to get back home.

"Audrey, I heard footsteps behind us when we were leaving. Do you think it's possible that we were seen?"

"I don't really think so. The bushes at the front of the house would have blocked the view of anyone at the front door. Plus, we were moving pretty fast."

After unpacking we decided to go back to get our bag and join the rest of the tour, but when we arrived back at the house that we had earlier escaped from, we found a crowd at the gated entrance and a security guard who wasn't letting anyone through. We walked up to the guard and explained to him that we were with the tour, but had been there earlier and that we just wanted to get our travel bag. He said that the crowd behind us was part of our tour and asked why we had been there before the rest of the group. He hesitated for a few minutes, then said he would see if we could go up to the house, so he radioed another security guard and explained the situation and told him to watch for us. As we walked back up the driveway, we noticed that there were only two cars now and they had 'caution' tape all around them. I wondered why the third car wasn't there and what the tape was all about. We got to the front door and explained to the second guard what had happened when we were there earlier and asked him what was going on. He said they were waiting for the police and that he couldn't tell us anything right now. Then he asked if I had any proof that the bag in the house belonged to me and said that we should wait there with him until the police arrived. Fortunately, the bag did have a tag on it with my name and address, and my drivers license would verify the address to show that the bag was mine. Our tour tickets had my address on them as well to prove that there was a reason for our being here.

The guard asked, "How did you get in the first time you were here, because the guard who was scheduled to be here to unlock the house and check everyone who went in had called in sick? I was called to come in and replace him."

"When we first arrived, the gate and the door were both un-locked and open, so we thought it might be okay to go in and wait for the rest of the tour to show up."

"Well, the gate and the house were both supposed to have been locked and there is a security code that has to be initiated to unlock each one."

Just then we saw two police cars coming up the driveway. The officers got out and started walking towards us. One of them asked the guard who we were and why we were here. The guard pulled one of the officers aside and told him what we had related to him about our being here and explained what he had found at the scene when he got there. The officer told the guard to find out where we left our bag and to get it and bring it to him. More officers arrived and were going into and around the perimeter of the house. The guard came out of the house and walked over to the first officer, who we found out was actually a detective, and spoke to him briefly before they both walked over to us.

"I'm Detective Ryan and said the security guard just told me that he didn't find a bag where we said we left it. Are you sure you left the bag at the foot of the stairs, Ms Simms?"

Audrey and I both looked at each other wide-eyed and not really knowing what to think.

"Yes, I'm sure of it. Are you sure it wasn't there?"

The detective told us to stay there with the guard while he went inside to look around for himself and get an update from the officers inside.

When he returned, he said, "I'll need to see some identification from both of you." We handed him our driver's licenses which he took over to his car. We assumed he was doing a criminal check on us to see if we had any records.

When he came back, we both asked together "What's going on?"

But before he could answer, another officer came up and said, "We checked out the two cars in the driveway and one belongs to the owner of the house, and the other belongs to the owner's real estate agent, Marsha Roberts."

I was so flustered by all that was going on that I didn't think to tell him that there had been three cars in the driveway when we left.

"I'll need both of your tour tickets. I see that you live out of town, but I'd like you to stay here for a few days while I investigate this a little further and I'll need a number where I can reach you."

Audrey spoke up as I handed him my business card with my cell phone on it. "What is going on? Are we being suspected of something?"

"You're not necessarily being suspected of anything, but you were at a crime scene and seem to be somehow involved."

"What's the crime? I think we should at least know that?"

"There was a murder here and I believe that it may have occurred during the time you were on the premises. I'm going to need a written and signed statement from both of you, stating exactly what happened the first time you were here, from the time you arrived until the time you left. I'm going to want to talk to you both again later because, so far, I can't find any information on there being a home tour here or at any of the other houses listed on the tickets that my officer already picked up."

Audrey and I were escorted back to the gate in a state of shock. Audrey looked puzzled and simply asked "Murder?"

As we neared the gate, we saw an officer gathering more tour tickets from the group outside the gate and writing down information on everyone. We guessed they had been told that there was never a tour and that they had probably been scammed because there were looks of shock and anger on a lot of their faces. We also spotted reporters and camera crews arriving from the local newspapers and TV stations.

By this time, it was early afternoon and we were starving, so we drove up to a small sidewalk café for some lunch and a much desired glass of wine. As we sat there eating lunch in a fog-like state of mind, not believing what we had just experienced, I asked Audrey "Do you know just how lucky we were to have gotten out of there when we did? Do you realize the possibilities of what could have happened if the murderer had seen us?"

As we talked about the possibilities of what could have happened if the people that were arguing knew we were there, I remembered that the security guard said our bag was not where we had left it. What if the murderer picked up the bag that had my address tag on it? If he or she did, that means he/she may know that someone else was in the house while they were there and they now knew where that someone lives. Suddenly, I felt sick to my stomach as I told Audrey about my realization.

Audrey assured me, "You're just letting your imagination run rampant. They'll probably find it in the house in another location." She was probably right and I was just worrying for nothing.

Audrey added, "It's too early to go back to the hotel just to sit around and wait. What do you say we find the Real Estate office that sponsored the tour and see if anyone else in the office knew what was going on?"

The café we were in offered internet connection, so I went to the car to get my laptop. I did a search and easily found the office location, which was only a mile from where we were.

When we arrived at the office, the only one there was the receptionist.

"Hi, come on in. My name's Becky Jones. How can I help you?"

"Hi, Becky! We purchased tickets for a Celebrity Home Tour that was sponsored by your office and we were wondering what you might know about it."

Becky suddenly became very nervous and teary-eyed. "The police were here asking the same thing and told me not to talk to anyone, but I don't know anything about it, anyway. All I do know is that a man kept calling for her yesterday and he was extremely angry about something."

"Did you tell that to the police when they were here?"

"No. I actually forgot about it until just now, but I should probably call and let Detective Ryan know."

"We'll be talking to Detective Ryan later today and we can let him know for you."

Before we could get back to our hotel, I got a call from Detective Ryan asking to meet with us in the hotel lobby.

As soon as we met, he started in with the interrogating. "I'd like you both to tell me in detail everything that happened after you arrived at the house. I'm going to record our conversations, but I still need to get everything in writing. Okay, so let's just start with your arrival at the house."

We both told him everything we could think of. Then I remembered about the third car. "I was in such shock when we talked at the house that I neglected to tell you that there were three cars in the driveway when we left the first time."

He said he wasn't aware that there had been a third car and immediately got on his phone to have the crime scene investigators check for tire marks from a third vehicle. I also told him about our visit to the Real Estate office and what Becky had mentioned to us about the angry man who had been calling.

As he was walking out the door, he mentioned, "We still haven't found any travel bag, but before you head back home, I'll contact the police where you live to have them keep an eye on your house."

Needless to say, I didn't sleep well that night. I phoned in to our assistant at the office to let her know we would be gone a few more days than we had anticipated.

"Hi, Jenny. I just wanted to call to let you know that we are going to be staying a few more days."

"Okay." Jenny responded. "By the way, some man keeps calling here asking for you, but won't leave a message or give his name. Maybe you have a secret admirer."

I had a bad feeling about who it might be and he was, definitely, no admirer. I turned to Audrey and said, "I just talked to Jenny at the office, and she said a guy has been calling there for me, but won't leave a name or message. This is really starting to worry me."

After breakfast, I called Detective Ryan to see if they had any new information and to tell him that we would be able to stay a few more days. He said they haven't been able to locate Joseph, the security guard who had called in sick, and that they traced the information from the tour tickets to the real estate agent's website and it seems there was indeed a scam going on. At that point he let us know that it was the real estate agent, Marsha Roberts, who had been killed.

He then asked if I thought I would recognize the voices that I heard at the house if I heard them again.

"I think I might be able to recognize them, but when I heard the voices at the house they were almost yelling, so I don't know if they would sound the same at a different pitch. I'll be happy to try, though."

He asked us to come down to the police station. When we got there, he played a tape and asked if the voice sounded familiar. The female voice was loud and angry and I told him that it was, in fact, one of the voices that I had heard. He said that was the voice of Marsha Roberts, the Realtor who was killed, and she apparently had a bit of a temper. Then he played another tape of a voice that I didn't recognize and that was the voice of the owner of the house. He laughed and said he was surprised that I didn't recognize the voice because it was that of a well-known celebrity that they were still trying to contact. He didn't say who the celebrity was, but we were sure it was probably all over the morning paper (which we hadn't seen yet). Reporters have ways of finding things out who lives where. An officer opened the door and interrupted us saying they just brought in Joseph Stallworth, the missing security guard, who they found at the airport. He asked if we could wait there while he questioned him.

After about an hour, he returned and told us it was okay for us to go home now. He said they thought they had things pretty well figured out.

I asked, "Was it the missing security guard who picked up my travel bag and did he have it on him? I won't feel comfortable going home not knowing if someone else has that bag and knows where to find me."

He said, "I don't know yet and I have a few things to check out, but I'll get in touch with you as soon as I have something substantial to tell you."

We were relaxing by the pool at the hotel when he called and said they found my travel bag, but needed to send it to the lab for fingerprinting. He said he would have to send it to me when they were done. He also summed up for us what had happened.

"In a nutshell, Joseph Stallworth, the security guard who we picked up at the airport, had befriended Marsha Roberts because she was very well known as an outstanding Realtor in the community and had listed and sold a lot of properties that he kept watch over. His car was the third car that you saw at the scene. He and the owner of the house left in it before you got back to the house the second time. I'm not sure where the idea originated, but Marsha put an ad on her website promoting the Celebrity Home Tour, figuring no one would question it because she had such a good reputation in the community. They knew things had to be kept quiet and done quickly. Apparently you, as well as the other people who were scammed, were on some sort of email list that linked to her website. Everything was set up to ensure that the tour appeared to be legitimate. Anyway, the plan was that they would split the money that was made from selling the tour tickets. That simple plan was changed when Joseph found out that the owner of the first house was going to be out of town, at which point the plan changed to include robbery and an escape out of the country. We found airline tickets on top of his bedroom dresser for him and Marsha. The celebrity-owner, who was supposed to be out of town walked in on them and confronted the guard, who told her everything and said it had been Marsha's idea and that she had planned it all. The owner and Marsha got into an argument which turned physical and that's when she was killed. To keep the guard quiet and from turning her in, the owner promised to take him out of the country and treat him to a life of luxury, which is why we found him at the airport. We still haven't located the owner, but we will. At this point, we're not sure about his involvement, if there even was any. So, you're free to go home now and can read the details in the newspaper and the police report that I'll send you. I figure you deserve to get a copy after what you've both been through. Don't worry, I'll have constant security around you and your house until this is all cleared up."

They looked at each other with relief and knew this was one business trip they would always remember. When they returned home and their friends asked them how the home tour was, they were really going to have a story to tell them!

✗

THE PECULIAR ADVENTURE OF THE PARADOL CHAMBER

by Jack Grochot

Sherlock Holmes was engaged in a complicated discussion with our tobacconist about the distinctive ash of an imported Virginia and Latakia mixture, while I was casually examining the briar of a new Peterson pipe. "It is the combination of these colours that separates this blend from others," Holmes remarked, referring to an observation in his monograph on the topic of the various ashes. Soon he purchased eight ounces of his favourite shag tobacco, and with a sweeping motion toward me announced that it was time to go. "The hands of Big Ben have crept forward while we were stationary in this aromatic shop," said he, adding: "If we are not to be late for our rendezvous, we must depart the premises immediately."

We were outside moments later in the bitter cold of a February afternoon in the year 1890, my long astrakhan topcoat buttoned at the collar to keep the scarf tucked against my neck. Sherlock Holmes wore his plaid frock coat without a scarf and seemed comfortable enough, but while we waited for a hansom at the corner he bounced up and down rapidly to aid his circulation. The cab came toward us with a lurch, one wheel striking a rut in the frozen mud. The horse's shoes clanked on the hard earth, as if the animal were trotting on cobblestone pavement. "Aldgate Station," Holmes barked to the coachman. We would connect there to the Underground and arrive at Howe Street, a block from the Diogenes Club, where we would meet up with Mycroft Holmes, the older brother of Sherlock Holmes and the person who would introduce us to our three o'clock appointment.

Sherlock Holmes knocked at the club's main door with five minutes to spare, and we were ushered in at the mention of Mycroft Holmes's name. The doorman being new, he did not recognize Sherlock Holmes as a repeat visitor and guest of his brother. I, too, was admitted after the doorman was informed that I had been invited by Mycroft Holmes as an assistant in matters of importance.

We could only assume this was an occasion of great import because Mycroft Holmes was about to introduce us to Martin Yant, a deputy Home Secretary with whom he served under the Prime Minister.

We entered the Stranger's room, furnished with modern sofas, soft armchairs, and mahogany desks. Sherlock Holmes's brother was seated with his legs crossed on a settee, his fidgety colleague next to him. They both stood as soon as we went in.

"Well, Sherlock, you are prompt as usual—and a fortunate thing it is, because Mr Yant cannot be kept waiting today," began Mycroft Holmes, noting that Yant was engaged in a timely project that demanded much of his attention. Yant wasted not an instant in broaching his problem.

"Mr Holmes," he addressed Sherlock, with a voice hardly above a whisper, "our country is depending on you to solve a rather perplexing international mystery." Yant's bow tie bounced on his Adam's apple as he spoke. "The Empire is engulfed in a dispute between two of our valued trading partners abroad, China and Japan, both struggling for regional dominance in East Asia. The conflict could result in a catastrophe, war, and to avert such a devastating blow to Britain's economy, we at the Home Office sent a seasoned mediator to negotiate a peaceful settlement between the Qing Dynasty and the Meiji.

"When he returned to London, sooner than we thought possible, the man reported to us nothing about any negotiations. Rather, he talked of his childhood, of a woman he loved, of a book he was reading, and of other nonsense. In short, he came back a blithering idiot. At first we thought he had simply lost his mind, and we found him a therapist. But the story does not end there, regrettably.

"We culled through our personnel files and located a suitable substitute for our agent. We sent the second mediator on the same mission, and when he returned, he was in the identical condition!

"Mr Holmes, we are at a standstill and the clock is ticking toward belligerence. We suspect espionage by a hostile government to prevent our efforts from succeeding."

Sherlock Holmes wanted to know who would profit from a failure, and Yant was bereft of an answer. "That is what we were hoping you would discover," Yant told him.

"But why me and not one of your own operatives?" Holmes asked, acting as if he were expendable but inviting a flattering response:

"We fear our own people are under surveillance and would meet with unfavourable results, where you, Mr Holmes, possess the cunning and stealth to wrap this package into a neat bundle while preserving your anonymity."

"I would never risk disappointing the Crown, so I willingly take on this challenging assignment, no matter how deep the waters," Holmes said humbly.

With that, we exchanged pleasant adieus and went our separate ways, Holmes to Baker Street and I back to my diggings in Kensington.

The next day, at about one o'clock, a messenger delivered a terse note from Holmes. He was summoning me to the Home Secretary's headquarters, where he had set up consecutive interviews of the two curiously confused mediators who were now confined to inside duty. Holmes wanted my medical knowledge to influence the questioning. The pair still had no recollection of any official functions or endeavours, but each used an unfamiliar word when referring to their experiences in China: the word Paradol, they recalled, had special meaning, in the context of something terrifying.

Later, Sherlock Holmes and I ate dinner at Simpson's—broiled chicken, baked potatoes, and baby peas—and before the succulent meal was served, we briefly discussed the case over a glass of muscatel wine. Holmes was intrigued by the puzzle of who might stand to gain from Sino-Japanese combat over control of Korea. He came to the conclusion, after careful reasoning and with me as a sounding board, that the culprit or unfriendly nation was likely to repeat the clandestine methods if the Home Office persisted in its efforts.

"What do you make of the mental state of the two Home Office emissaries?" I implored. "Could it be they were the unwitting victims of a devious trick that would cause them to forget their purpose—or could it be, heaven forbid, bribery?"

"Watson, I must congratulate you for your deductive prowess," Holmes shot back. "But, as I have said before, it is a capital mistake to theorise before you have all the facts. It biases the judgment. I must have data so as not to twist facts to suit a theory."

Eventually, the conversation drifted toward mundane topics.

After dinner, we occupied two armchairs at his apartment, pulling them close to the fireplace, with our stocking feet resting on the warm bearskin hearthrug. I took up a copy of that evening's *Standard* and Holmes became engrossed in his Index, an encyclopedia he had compiled with docketed information on criminals, arms dealers, luminaries, spies, underworld characters, scientific experts, things, and subjects. He was researching his entries without a word for at least two hours, when: "Watson," he intoned, "for one reason or another I have eliminated all possibilities but one." He said no more.

The hour drew late, so I prepared to leave for my quarters as Holmes began to pace up and down the room, his hands clasped behind his back, his chin on his chest, and his brows furrowed, as was his custom when lost in thought.

In the mid-morning of the following day, in my consulting room, I treated an elderly gentleman, a new patient, who complained of a continuous pain in his rectum. After a few simple queries and an examination, I diagnosed the ailment as a prostate infection and prescribed a medication along with hot soakings in the tub. In a matter of a few minutes after he was gone, grateful that his problem was not too serious, there came an agitated knocking at the door.

It was Sherlock Holmes, breathless.

"Once again, the game is afoot, Watson," said he. Next came an entreaty. "Watson, I need you to accompany me on a trip to Peking, where the two Home Office agents encountered their trouble. Could you please contact Dr Anstruther and ask him to take over your practice for a time, because we may be away for a considerable period? We should leave this evening."

I did not hesitate. "I can clear my schedule and be ready by this afternoon," I responded.

"Very well indeed," he said in reaction to my eagerness, adding: "I anticipated your cooperation and booked passage for us on the

Queen Victoria, which is sailing for Hong Kong at six o'clock. From there we will board a series of trains to our destination."

Holmes explained he already had enlisted the cooperation of Deputy Secretary Yant, who would dispatch yet a third emissary to Peking, this time making no secret of his objective. That would entice another attempt at thwarting the talks. Holmes and I were to team up to observe the agent's every move and apprehend the provocateurs.

Sherlock Holmes left in a rush, preoccupied with a task, about which he gave me no particulars.

Dr Anstruther, who regularly filled in for me when I was off on an adventure as Holmes's confederate, was enthused as usual to take my place. And so I made further preparations to leave, later riding a cab to Metropolitan Station for the Underground to the harbour at the end of Broad Street, where the *Queen Victoria* was docked.

Earlier, Holmes had been introduced discreetly at the Home Office to Robert LeRoch, the third agent, and late that afternoon followed him all the way to the steamship.

After my baggage was stowed in our cabin, which was one door from LeRoch's, just as Holmes had reserved them, I joined Sherlock Holmes on deck. He pointed out LeRoch to me and I made a note of his attire and description. He was distinguishable in a crowd, about five feet, nine inches tall with a pot belly and a swollen red face. Probably around fifty years old, he had a full white beard that was neatly clipped, and large, dark eyes that were set far apart. His hair, cropped short, was also white and parted in the centre. He wore a grey wool overcoat with the collar pulled up to his protruding ears, and heavy brown boots with a broad metal heel. That he didn't don a hat or a cap in this inclement weather was worth marking down in my memory. If anyone else was watching him I could not detect it.

Thick, black smoke began to billow from the funnels, and the steam engines whined—the *Queen Victoria* had embarked on our voyage, about fifteen minutes late.

We waited for LeRoch to exit the deck and go to his cabin, both of us never letting him out of our view, acutely aware that an attack could come at any moment. Instead of making his way to the cabin compartment, however, LeRoch found the dining room and seated himself at a small table, for it was the peak of the supper hour. Holmes and I occupied a table for two within earshot of LeRoch before any more of the numerous passengers came in. Before long there was a waiting line. Holmes, who habitually deprived himself of food when intense on a case, nonetheless ordered a bit to eat—a grilled ham sandwich with a salad of mixed greens. I had skipped lunch and was famished, so I chose a slice of baked ham, scalloped potatoes, broccoli with cheese sauce, and a portion of apple pie for dessert, topped with custard.

We shared a carafe of half-and-half before we were served our meal, and the waiter brought us our plates at the same time he cheerfully placed one in front of LeRoch. I noticed no other person sitting alone, except for a lovely young woman, producing no indication that LeRoch was the target of our enemy's attention. Regardless, Holmes was pensive. That night he was restless and he rejected my offer to stand watch while he got some sleep, fitful though it might have been.

I rested soundly for almost six hours, and in the morning Holmes listened for the sound of LeRoch's door closing on his way to breakfast. Afterward, we spent a few minutes on deck, but the nasty headwinds were so chilling they chased us back to our cozy cabins.

Days of boredom set in, I sporadically perusing medical journals that had been overlooked for some time and Holmes full-heartedly polishing a magazine article he was writing about the differences in fibers when viewed through a magnifying glass. The entire journey was uneventful, save for some rough seas and my attending to a middle-aged stock broker who had symptoms of lung disease. He was on his honeymoon and my prognosis ruined his and his bride's outlook for the future. I recommended a specialist I knew in London if the broker wanted a second opinion that might on the off-chance disagree with mine.

Finally, our steamship arrived at the port of Hong Kong, not long after Holmes was convinced an assault of some nature could occur on the trains or in Peking, but more likely in the capital city. We learned after disembarking from the steamship that we had to wait in the teeming metropolis for two days to catch our transportation through much of the expansive country. The narrow-gauge railways to Peking ran only on odd days for the day and-a-half trip. So, we rode the new Rising Star ferry across the choppy bay to Kowloon and bought our train tickets at Hung Hom station. On our return to Hong Kong, we took a rickshaw behind LeRoch's to the nearest decent hotel. Little did we know there was another rickshaw in back of ours that was en-route to the same place, the Qang Si Palace, built by the Bombay opium exporter Dorabjee Naorojee. Foreigners in Hong Kong for the first time, both Holmes and I were infatuated by the bustling activity on the immaculate streets. Throngs of tiny people criss-crossed in front of us, dashing to colourfully-decorated shops and hum-drum dwellings, outside of which hung laundry and linens on balcony clotheslines.

When the coolie pulling the rickshaw deposited us at the door-step of the hotel, Holmes paid him with shillings, which he was satisfied to earn, and we entered the sparsely-furnished lobby to register for a room next to LeRoch's. The desk clerk obliged and gave us a key to accommodations with one bedroom on the second floor. So far we had experienced no language barrier, because the merchants were accustomed to British guests, Colonial Hong Kong being a multi-ethnic crossroads of commerce and tourism.

After we all dined on a seafood menu at a restaurant kitty-corner from the hotel, we retired for the night, but I couldn't help but notice the lovely young woman from the ship at a far corner of the establishment. She was finished with her supper, lounging at a table with a newspaper spread in front of her.

The wait for the first of the connecting trains to Peking passed without incident, and so we climbed the steps to a busy carriage toward the rear, the same attractive lady taking a seat next to Le-Roch just as the locomotive wheels began to screech and grind. The pair engaged in casual conversation when the train picked up speed. It was not difficult to guess that she had shown a keen interest in LeRoch, without appearing to be uncommonly forward. She dressed provocatively: a tight-fitting tan blouse with pearls on the cuffs under her unbuttoned waistcoat revealed an ample bosom. A pleated green skirt accented her shapely hips and thighs, and pastel patent-leather boots with a moderately high heel matched the skirt. It was obvious LeRoch was impressed by her beauty.

In the morning, she was nowhere to be seen, but LeRoch glanced around the car in an apparent effort to locate her. We could see out the window the fast-moving landscape. It was replete with verdant rice patties and lush farmlands, purple snow-capped mountain ranges, and yellow rocky plateaus.

The fourth train we had ridden pulled into the station in Peking late in the evening, and we found a swank hotel, The Chang Su Son, which displayed an ornate fountain out front and an elaborate vegetable garden along the side. It was there that she surfaced again, just after we had signed in. LeRoch and she greeted each other cordially, like long-lost acquaintances, and they took more than a few minutes to renew their relationship on a flowery sofa that provided privacy. Holmes and I aimlessly meandered through the lobby, pausing at the foot of all the magnificent paintings, until LeRoch's comely companion politely excused herself, checked in, and went up to her room. LeRoch remained on the divan, gazing at her fondly until she disappeared from sight. Holmes peeked at the register to learn her name: Laura Cable—if that was her true identity. Miss Cable, as it turned out, had selected a suite across the hall from LeRoch.

Once we were settled for the night, Holmes cracked open our door so he could have a perfect vantage point to take in any activity at Miss Cable's room and LeRoch's. Holmes slid a desk chair to the opening, sat down, and pushed the chair onto its back legs against the wall, letting his feet dangle. In that semi-reclining position he could both relax and observe anything in the hallway that stirred. "I dare not doze off during this vigil, despite a tiring day," he remarked, and promised to allow me to relieve him at two o'clock in the morning.

But it never got that late before something sinister occurred.

About midnight, Holmes gently shook me out of dreamland to say in a hushed tone that Miss Cable, carrying a brandy decanter, had rapped softly on LeRoch's door and gone in. For certain he had been expecting her. The partitions between the rooms were paper thin and we could hear the two giggling next to us. There was conversation, but we couldn't make out the words, only the voices of a woman and a man, in addition to the tinkle of glass when they poured more drink. The frivolity went on for a quarter of an hour until we heard LeRoch groan briefly, after which came the ominous sound of a heavy body collapsing onto the floor with a thud.

My initial instinct was to rush over to assist, but Holmes stopped me in my stride. "Wait to see what transpires," he insisted quietly, "for I believe we are at the onset of a subversive plan." He presumed correctly, because it wasn't long before Holmes beckoned me to the slit in the door and together we watched Miss Cable tip-toe out of LeRoch's room to make her way down the hall to the back stairs. There, she waved her hand and was joined by four Chinamen who had been waiting on the landing for her signal. They scurried silently behind her toward LeRoch's suite and quickly walked in, single-file. We heard muffled sounds of their struggle to lift LeRoch and soon saw them convey him, un-conscious, by the legs and arms back toward the end of the hallway leading to the stairs, Miss Cable trailing.

"On the double, Watson, fetch our coats and hats before we lose this gang," Holmes commanded as they vanished at the top of the steps. "She slipped him a drug in his brandy," Holmes surmised as we descended the curving stairway and heard the kidnappers reach the bottom. They paused at the rear entrance while Miss Cable held open the door and made sure the coast was clear. The short, narrow alley outside was deserted and the Chinamen clumsily carted the limp torso to a horse-drawn hearse. It was stationed at the end of the passage near the intersection of a street full of activity even at that hour. The stamina of these slightly-built miscreants astounded me as they raised their cumbersome cargo and shoved LeRoch into the tail section of the hearse, not very gently. Meanwhile, Miss Cable climbed aboard with the driver as Holmes and I hailed a sedan chair, borne by four coolies, to continue our pursuit. Holmes instructed our bearers in perfect Chinese, which Holmes had stud-ied in college, for each one of them shrugged his shoulders and gave us a blank stare when the sentences were spoken in English.

We kept at a safe distance to avoid being spotted, moving slowly, as if in a funeral procession. The journey covered several kilometers. When we reached a warehouse district near the Chang-pu River, the hearse pulled up to the front of a dilapidated brick structure that apparently had been abandoned, because the ground floor and first storey windows were boarded up, save for the ones on the door to the left and around the corner. Holmes and I jumped from the litter, paying the lead porter with a sovereign, and telling him to go on his way with his crew. We went on foot toward the concealment of an adjacent building and saw a large tin door in the front swing open, worked by someone inside, a tall, stout Caucasian. A more detailed description I couldn't manage at this juncture because the lighting at the front of the warehouse was insufficient. Miss Cable alighted from the hearse and had a few words with the stranger, then motioned to the driver to proceed. The hearse turned and went in, the bay door closing instantly behind it, the horse never shying.

Holmes and I crept up to the side door to catch a glimpse of the action inside, careful not to be seen through the filthy windows. The interior was vacant, except for the occupants, the hearse, and the oddest-looking object in the centre of the floor. It was a small chamber, with enough space in it to house a human being. In the shape of a pentagon, it was constructed of polished steel framework and glass walls, with a megaphone embedded to carry sound inward. A wooden office chair was visible, as was a pinwheel at eye level directly in front of the chair.

"We'll stay here and watch what goes on before we make our move, Watson, but surely before any harm comes to LeRoch," said Holmes as he stood aloof from the situation, much like a surgeon who coolly restrains his emotions when ready to use the knife. "I trust you brought along your old service revolver," he added as an afterthought. I nodded and brought the grip end out of my overcoat pocket to reassure him.

In short order, Miss Cable and her ally went to the back of the hearse and began to coax LeRoch out of the conveyance. He was conscious now but unsteady, groggy. They placed their hands under his armpits and escorted him to the chamber. He more or less fell into the chair, perspiring profusely. They secured the latch and left him to recover further while they opened wide the bay door to permit the hearse to exit. There was ample space in the deserted building for the hearse to make a 180-degree turn and move out onto the dirt street. Miss Cable and her co-conspirator then closed the bay door. And the man went right to work, Miss Cable positioning herself in the background. Now we were able to discern his features under the glow of lanterns along the upper rim of the booth. He was about sixty years of age with a gaunt, wrinkly face and sunken eyes. His nose was bulbous and he had wide side whiskers that extended below his ear lobes. He wore a constant frown, and on the top of his head was an unkempt shock, reddish-brown flecked with grey. His clothing was that of a businessman.

He spoke into the megaphone—we could not hear what he was saying—and as he did, he operated a crank that sent the pinwheel spinning. The circular design on it turned like the threads of a screw. LeRoch stared at the pinwheel and wiped his forehead with his palm.

Holmes had witnessed enough. "Sound the bugle, Watson! Charge!" he bellowed, and abruptly flung open the side door to burst inside, I right behind him.

Startled, the man stood erect and confronted us. Miss Cable was motionless.

Before either could utter a word, Holmes, shouting, announced our intentions: "I am Sherlock Holmes and this is Dr John H Watson, here under the authority of the British Crown. Both of you are under arrest!"

The two were speechless as Holmes continued loudly. "We demand to know who you are and what you are doing."

The old criminal answered, stammering and making a feeble attempt to throw Holmes off course. "I am D-D-Doctor G-G-Geoffrey T-T-Tombe, hypnotherapist and British subject; the chap in the cubicle is my patient, and this is my nurse assistant. What are the charges?"

"Abducting a government agent and retarding his mission," Holmes retorted as he approached the chamber and sprung the latch to set LeRoch free. I, meanwhile, maintained a guard over our two prisoners, my right hand on the butt of the pistol. Out of the corner of my eye I noticed above the latch a small bronze plaque with raised letters, reading "1879 PARADOL Bros, Ltd, USA."

"You both have some explaining to do," said Holmes in a calm manner, "but I must warn you that anything you say will be taken down and could be used against you in court." He went on: "You, particularly, Miss Cable, are in a legal morass because of the premeditative nature of your conduct. It would be in your best interest to make a clean breast of this matter. Tell us with whom you are in league. I believe I already know the answer—the second most lethal villain in London."

She broke down, sobbing, but was reluctant to divulge the evidence. "Oh, Mr Holmes," she whimpered, "I was paid handsomely to do what I did, but if I give you the information I am as good as dead. My mother is gravely ill and I desperately needed the money for her care. Now she is doomed."

"Perhaps we can protect you, and help your mother, Miss Cable, but we can talk about that on the way to the British embassy," Holmes told her in a sympathetic tone.

We marched out into the early morning sunshine, LeRoch a few paces behind but sober. "I am indebted to you brave souls for my rescue," he said to Holmes and me as we reached the door.

"It was no bother at all," I responded, thinking later that it was a silly thing to say.

We proceeded to a populated avenue and hailed a coach after a lengthy wait with little discourse. LeRoch sat with Holmes and me across from Dr Tombe and Miss Cable, who confessed finally that she was an actress using her stage name. Her real name was Norma Uffelman and she said she had been hired in London for five hundred pounds plus expenses to play the part of LeRoch's femme fatale. But who had employed her remained undisclosed. LeRoch glared at her, not admiringly any more.

When Holmes explained our presence to the embassy receptionist, she sent a page boy to fetch a security officer, who took us to a section on the ground floor that contained four unoccupied jail cells. We showed Miss Uffelman into one and Dr Tombe into another, far apart so they couldn't connive. We left them there to stew awhile about their predicament. Holmes, LeRoch, and I then met with a Scotland Yard inspector, Roger Stuart, who was stationed at the embassy. Over breakfast we went through the elements of the case and developed a strategy for our next move.

Holmes said he already had come up with an idea to entrap whoever was behind the kidnapping, but he was mum about the details. Inspector Stuart said he would go along with anything Holmes intended, so long as Scotland Yard remained involved.

"We'll spring the trap on him and then Scotland Yard can expose the scandal to the newsies," Holmes chortled.

Holmes's plan depended almost entirely on the complicity of Miss Uffelman, who by the time we had returned to the cellblock was more receptive to Holmes's offer to protect her and help her mother. "Did you mean what you said about shielding me from retaliation for cooperating with you?" she asked meekly through the iron bars.

"Miss Uffelman," Holmes said somberly, "this affair with you and Dr Tombe is but a sub-plot to a grand play that could jeopardise the stability of the British Empire. The government can reward you with leniency for aiding us in solving this crime as well as make certain that your safety is not compromised.

"The Crown will go so far as to change your identity, re-locate you to, say, New York, and provide you with the opportunity to succeed on Broadway. And there in the city you would find competent medical services for your mother.

"That, of course, would require you to name the malefactor who paid you and testify against him."

Miss Uffelman's face brightened at the prospects. "Maybe I shall do as you ask," said she. "But first get me out of here."

"Not until we get the whole story from you, Miss Uffelman, a story we can use in a courtroom," Holmes said sternly.

"All right, then, Mr Holmes, I'll tell it to you from the beginning," she said compliantly.

She recalled how she had lived on a meager billet as an understudy at the Lyceum and Haymarket theatres, barely surviving on her own after spending large sums for her mother's care. One recent evening, she said, after a performance, a rugged-looking man, Tom Wheatley, nicknamed Boozer, went backstage and wanted to know if she needed a better acting job. She instantly answered in the affirmative, even though he told her the position would not involve the stage and could be hazardous. Boozer took her to a cafe at the intersection of Glasshouse and Regent streets, where she was introduced to her soon-to-be benefactor, a retired army colonel, Sebastian Moran. He was deceitful, she alleged, because he told her he was working with the Home Office to snare a double-agent, a traitor who was engaged in an act of betrayal that would reach a climax in Peking.

Colonel Moran probed to learn if she was capable of traveling to such a distant land, but she was reluctant because of her mother's condition. He pledged to hire a nurse to look after her mother while Miss Uffelman was gone, and then revealed the details of her role, producing the five hundred pounds as an enticement. She accepted his offer with a twinge of dread.

"Did he give you an address if you found it necessary to contact him?" Holmes asked.

"He said he could be reached again at the cafe," she answered.

"Are you prepared to go to court and repeat your narrative, Miss Uffelman?" Holmes wanted to know.

"I am, if you keep your word, Mr Holmes."

"My word is my bond, Miss Uffelman. This will go a long way in your favour," he concluded.

Dr Tombe, who had been taken to a room out of the cellblock so he couldn't eavesdrop on the conversation between Holmes and Miss Uffelman, proved to be a wealth of information also. It was all pertinent evidence, which, he said, he would repeat under oath at a trial.

"I am not a young man any more, Mr Holmes," he said to preface his account, "and a stretch in the penitentiary would be tantamount to a death sentence."

At first, he provided tidbits that an aggressive prosecutor could build into devastating evidence. As he related it, Dr Tombe and Colonel Moran had been friends since they met at a conference at the University of London, my alma mater for my medical degree. Dr Tombe and Colonel Moran stayed in touch and occasionally the two would have lunch or dinner together, and it was at one of those times that Colonel Moran proposed the role Dr Tombe played in the drama. Dr Tombe admitted that he had induced the first two agents to lose their grip on reality by imposing a hypnotic trance, in the same manner that he had attempted with LeRoch.

Dr Tombe's recompense was one thousand pounds each time he achieved the desired results.

"Your assistance will be duly noted at your sentencing," Sherlock Holmes assured him.

After we left the embassy, I asked Holmes why he hadn't been in the least surprised that Colonel Moran was the mastermind of the plot.

"I suspected my foe Moran nearly from the start," he revealed, continuing: "When I was consulting my Index back at Baker Street, I entertained the thought that if I ruled out a hostile government, only an international arms smuggler could profit from a war between China and Japan. Such an individual would possess the wherewithal and connections to accomplish a sale of munitions, as well as arrange for the intercession of Britain to end miserably. Colonel Moran fit the bill. Therefore, I spent the night devising a plan, and early in the morning, at dawn, I sent Mercer, my general utility man, to the Cafe Royal, where Moran gathers his henchmen and concocts his conspiracies. At exactly eight o'clock, two Orientals approached their table at the back wall and began an animated discussion with Moran. When it was almost over, Moran reached behind him, and from a cloth case he withdrew a new American military bolt-action rifle, which he demonstrated. The two visitors smiled broadly and nodded their heads excitedly. There was some jibber-jabber and they parted on good terms. I was certain a deal had been struck."

"And why were you not shocked at the method to incapacitate the mediators?" I wanted to learn.

"Simplicity itself, Watson. I merely remembered our dialogue just last year about the findings of the British Medical Association on the applications of hypnotherapy. I deduced that it surely could be employed for a Machiavellian outcome as well as for a healthy one," Holmes said.

Holmes and I returned to our hotel room while Inspector Stuart made arrangements with the China ambassador to file the appropriate documents to extradite the prisoners back to London.

"We must prove Moran had knowledge of the unlawful activity and coordinated it, too," Holmes stated.

"And how do you propose to do that?" I enquired.

"I intend to permit the man's genius and his ego to be his undoing—the colonel will tell us it is so in his own words," came his answer.

With that, Holmes withdrew a sheet of foolscap from the desk drawer and composed a cryptic message. He took time to be meticulous about the wording, re-wrote it twice, reviewed it, and finally was satisfied that it said exactly what he wanted. He showed it to me. It read:

> Colonel Moran -
> Plan gone awry. Subject rejected my advances. Please advise.

Respond to Chang Su Son Hotel, Peking.

It was signed "L Cable."

"We shall go to a telegraph office to send this wire to him in care of the Cafe Royal. And then, we wait," Holmes said, and he laughed in the noiseless fashion that was peculiar to him.

After our excursion to transmit the message, we got some rest and were visited by Inspector Stuart, who had been communicating with his superiors in London about the developments in the case. Inspector Stuart was amused by the wording of the telegram. "The reply to this wire might very well provide the corroboration we need for their testimony," he remarked. Later, the inspector identified himself to the hotel manager and instructed him to give any messages for Miss Cable to her associate, Sherlock Holmes.

A wire for her came the next afternoon. Holmes and I were passing through the lobby on our way back from lunch when a bellboy directed us to the main counter. The clerk handed Holmes a sealed envelope and asked that he see to it Miss Cable received it. We hurried to our room, and Holmes used his pocket knife to slit open the envelope. It contained a message from Colonel Moran. This is what it said:

> Laura -
> You are an actress. Give subject your best performance.
> Act! Failure unacceptable.

Holmes wrung his hands and danced a jig. "This should do him in!" he beamed.

Inspector Stuart set the wheels of justice in motion again, notifying his superiors that we had obtained the evidence necessary to take Colonel Moran into custody.

They did.

When we arrived on the train on our return trip to Hong Kong two days later, I bought a copy of *The Times* at the newsstand. The top right hand column displayed a full account of how Scotland Yard had disrupted a scheme to undermine the efforts of the British Home Office.

Later in the year, Miss Uffelman and Dr Tombe were given light sentences, short periods of probation. Miss Uffelman then vanished, it seemed, from the face of the earth.

Colonel Moran fared worse. After a trial that lasted a week, a jury found him guilty and he was ordered to serve one year of hard labour at Pentonville Prison, called The Dungeon by its inmates.

Colonel Moran vowed revenge against Sherlock Holmes as they led the arrogant convict, in shackles, out of the courtroom.

A month afterward, Holmes and I attended a concert of Franz Berwald compositions at Albert Hall. While waiting for the conductor to rap his baton, Holmes made a prophetic comment that one day came to haunt me: "Although a major instigator of evil is tucked away securely now at Pentonville, I doubt the duress he undergoes there will change his tune. I expect there will come a time when Colonel Sebastian Moran and I shall encounter each other once again."

THE RED-HEADED LEAGUE

by Sir Arthur Conan Doyle

I had called upon my friend, Mr. Sherlock Holmes, one day in the autumn of last year and found him in deep conversation with a very stout, florid-faced, elderly gentleman with fiery red hair. With an apology for my intrusion, I was about to withdraw when Holmes pulled me abruptly into the room and closed the door behind me.

"You could not possibly have come at a better time, my dear Watson," he said cordially.

"I was afraid that you were engaged."

"So I am. Very much so."

"Then I can wait in the next room."

"Not at all. This gentleman, Mr. Wilson, has been my partner and helper in many of my most successful cases, and I have no doubt that he will be of the utmost use to me in yours also."

The stout gentleman half rose from his chair and gave a bob of greeting, with a quick little questioning glance from his small fat-encircled eyes.

"Try the settee," said Holmes, relapsing into his armchair and putting his fingertips together, as was his custom when in judicial moods. "I know, my dear Watson, that you share my love of all that is bizarre and outside the conventions and humdrum routine of everyday life. You have shown your relish for it by the enthusiasm which has prompted you to chronicle, and, if you will excuse my saying so, somewhat to embellish so many of my own little adventures."

"Your cases have indeed been of the greatest interest to me," I observed.

"You will remember that I remarked the other day, just before we went into the very simple problem presented by Miss Mary Sutherland, that for strange effects and extraordinary combinations we must go to life itself, which is always far more daring than any effort of the imagination."

"A proposition which I took the liberty of doubting."

"You did, Doctor, but none the less you must come round to my view, for otherwise I shall keep on piling fact upon fact on you until your reason breaks down under them and acknowledges me to be right. Now, Mr. Jabez Wilson here has been good enough to call upon me this morning, and to begin a narrative which promises to be one of the most singular which I have listened to for some time. You have heard me remark that the strangest and most unique things are very often connected not with the larger but with the smaller crimes, and occasionally, indeed, where there is room for doubt whether any positive crime has been committed. As far as I have heard it is impossible for me to say whether the present case is an instance of crime or not, but the course of events is certainly among the most singular that I have ever listened to. Perhaps, Mr. Wilson, you would have the great kindness to recommence your narrative. I ask you not merely because my friend Dr. Watson has not heard the opening part but also because the peculiar nature of the story makes me anxious to have every possible detail from your lips. As a rule, when I have heard some slight indication of the course of events, I am able to guide myself by the thousands of other similar cases which occur to my memory. In the present instance I am forced to admit that the facts are, to the best of my belief, unique."

The portly client puffed out his chest with an appearance of some little pride and pulled a dirty and wrinkled newspaper from the inside pocket of his greatcoat. As he glanced down the advertisement column, with his head thrust forward and the paper flattened out upon his knee, I took a good look at the man and endeavored, after the fashion of my companion, to read the indications which might be presented by his dress or appearance.

I did not gain very much, however, by my inspection. Our visitor bore every mark of being an average commonplace British tradesman, obese, pompous, and slow. He wore rather baggy gray shepherd's check trousers, a not over-clean black frock-coat, unbuttoned in the front, and a drab waistcoat with a heavy brassy Albert chain, and a square pierced bit of metal dangling down as an ornament. A frayed top-hat and a faded brown overcoat with a wrinkled velvet collar lay upon a chair beside him. Altogether, look as I would, there was nothing remarkable about the man save his blazing red head, and the expression of extreme chagrin and discontent upon his features.

Sherlock Holmes's quick eye took in my occupation, and he shook his head with a smile as he noticed my questioning glances. "Beyond the obvious facts that he has at some time done manual labour, that he takes snuff, that he is a Freemason, that he has been in China, and that he has done a considerable amount of writing lately, I can deduce nothing else."

Mr. Jabez Wilson started up in his chair, with his forefinger upon the paper, but his eyes upon my companion.

"How, in the name of good-fortune, did you know all that, Mr. Holmes?" he asked. "How did you know, for example, that I did manual labour. It's as true as gospel, for I began as a ship's carpenter."

"Your hands, my dear sir. Your right hand is quite a size larger than your left. You have worked with it, and the muscles are more developed."

"Well, the snuff, then, and the Freemasonry?"

"I won't insult your intelligence by telling you how I read that, especially as, rather against the strict rules of your order, you use an arc-and-compass breastpin."

"Ah, of course, I forgot that. But the writing?"

"What else can be indicated by that right cuff so very shiny for five inches, and the left one with the smooth patch near the elbow where you rest it upon the desk?"

"Well, but China?"

"The fish that you have tattooed immediately above your right wrist could only have been done in China. I have made a small study of tattoo marks and have even contributed to the literature of the subject. That trick of staining the fishes' scales of a delicate pink is quite peculiar to China. When, in addition, I see a Chinese coin hanging from your watch-chain, the matter becomes even more simple."

Mr. Jabez Wilson laughed heavily. "Well, I never!" said he. "I thought at first that you had done something clever, but I see that there was nothing in it, after all."

"I begin to think, Watson," said Holmes, "that I make a mistake in explaining. 'Omne ignotum pro magnifico,' you know, and my poor little reputation, such as it is, will suffer shipwreck if I am so candid. Can you not find the advertisement, Mr. Wilson?"

"Yes, I have got it now," he answered with his thick red finger planted halfway down the column. "Here it is. This is what began it all. You just read it for yourself, sir."

I took the paper from him and read as follows.

> TO THE RED-HEADED LEAGUE: On account of the bequest of the late Ezekiah Hopkins, of Lebanon, Pennsylvania, U. S. A., there is now another vacancy open which entitles a member of the League to a salary of 4 pounds a week for purely nominal services. All red-headed men who are sound in body and mind and above the age of twenty-one years, are eligible. Apply in person on Monday, at eleven o'clock, to Duncan Ross, at the offices of the League, 7 Pope's Court, Fleet Street.

"What on earth does this mean?" I ejaculated after I had twice read over the extraordinary announcement.

Holmes chuckled and wriggled in his chair, as was his habit when in high spirits. "It is a little off the beaten track, isn't it?" said he. "And now, Mr. Wilson, off you go at scratch and tell us all about yourself, your household, and the effect which this advertisement had upon your fortunes. You will first make a note, Doctor, of the paper and the date."

"It is *The Morning Chronicle* of April 27, 1890. Just two months ago."

"Very good. Now, Mr. Wilson?"

"Well, it is just as I have been telling you, Mr. Sherlock Holmes," said Jabez Wilson, mopping his forehead; "I have a small pawnbroker's business at Coburg Square, near the City. It's not a very large affair, and of late years it has not done more than just give me a living. I used to be able to keep two assistants, but now I only keep one; and I would have a job to pay him but that he is willing to come for half wages so as to learn the business."

"What is the name of this obliging youth?" asked Sherlock Holmes.

"His name is Vincent Spaulding, and he's not such a youth, either. It's hard to say his age. I should not wish a smarter assistant, Mr. Holmes; and I know very well that he could better himself and earn twice what I am able to give him. But, after all, if he is satisfied, why should I put ideas in his head?"

"Why, indeed? You seem most fortunate in having an employee who comes under the full market price. It is not a common experience among employers in this age. I don't know that your assistant is not as remarkable as your advertisement."

"Oh, he has his faults, too," said Mr. Wilson. "Never was such a fellow for photography. Snapping away with a camera when he ought to be improving his mind, and then diving down into the cellar like a rabbit into its hole to develop his pictures. That is his main fault, but on the whole he's a good worker. There's no vice in him."

"He is still with you, I presume?"

"Yes, sir. He and a girl of fourteen, who does a bit of simple cooking and keeps the place clean — that's all I have in the house, for I am a widower and never had any family. We live very quietly, sir, the three of us; and we keep a roof over our heads and pay our debts, if we do nothing more.

"The first thing that put us out was that advertisement. Spaulding, he came down into the office just this day eight weeks, with this very paper in his hand, and he says:

"'I wish to the Lord, Mr. Wilson, that I was a red-headed man.'

"'Why that?' I asks.

"'Why,' says he, 'here's another vacancy on the League of the Red-headed Men. It's worth quite a little fortune to any man who gets it, and I understand that there are more vacancies than there are men, so that the trustees are at their wits' end what to do with the money. If my hair would only change color, here's a nice little crib all ready for me to step into.'

"'Why, what is it, then?' I asked. You see. Mr. Holmes, I am a very stay-at-home man, and as my business came to me instead of my having to go to it, I was often weeks on end without putting my foot over the door-mat. In that way I didn't know much of what was going on outside, and I was always glad of a bit of news.

"'Have you never heard of the League of the Red-headed Men?' he asked with his eyes open.

"'Never.'

"'Why, I wonder at that, for you are eligibile yourself for one of the vacancies.'

"'And what are they worth?' I asked.

"'Oh, merely a couple of hundred a year, but the work is slight, and it need not interfere very much with one's other occupations.'

"Well, you can easily think that that made me prick up my ears, for the business has not been over-good for some years, and an extra couple of hundred would have been very handy.

"'Tell me all about it,' said I.

"'Well' said he, showing me the advertisement, 'you can see for yourself that the League has a vacancy, and there is the address where you should apply for particulars. As far as I can make out, the League was founded by an American millionaire, Ezekiah Hopkins, who was very peculiar in his ways. He was himself red-headed, and he had a great sympathy for all red-headed men; so when he died it was found that he had left his enormous fortune in the hands of trustees, with instructions to apply the interest to the providing of easy berths to men whose hair is of that color. From all I hear it is splendid pay and very little to do.'

"'But,' said I, 'there would be millions of red-headed men who would apply.'

"'Not so many as you might think,' he answered. 'You see it is really confined to Londoners, and to grown men. This American had started from London when he was young, and he wanted to do the old town a good turn. Then, again, I have heard it is no use your applying if your hair is light red, or dark red, or anything but real bright, blazing, fiery red. Now, if you cared to apply, Mr. Wilson, you would just walk in; but perhaps it would hardly be worth your while to put yourself out of the way for the sake of a few hundred pounds.'

"Now, it is a fact, gentlemen, as you may see for yourselves, that my hair is of a very full and rich tint, so that it seemed to me that if there was to be any competition in the matter I stood as good a chance as any man that I had ever met. Vincent Spaulding seemed to know so much about it that I thought he might prove useful, so I just ordered him to put up the shutters for the day and to come right away with me. He was very willing to have a holiday, so we shut the business up and started off for the address that was given us in the advertisement.

"I never hope to see such a sight as that again, Mr. Holmes. From north, south, east, and west every man who had a shade of red in his hair had tramped into the city to answer the advertise-ment. Fleet Street was choked with red-headed folk, and Pope's Court looked like a coster's orange barrow. I should not have thought there were so many in the whole country as were brought together by that single advertisement. Every shade of color they were—straw, lemon, orange, brick, Irish-setter, liver, clay; but, as Spaulding said, there were not many who had the real vivid flame-colored tint. When I saw how many were waiting, I would have given it up in despair; but Spaulding would not hear of it. How he did it I could not imagine, but he pushed and pulled and butted until he got me through the crowd, and right up to the steps which led to the office. There was a double stream upon the stair, some going up in hope, and some coming back dejected; but we wedged in as well as we could and soon found ourselves in the office."

"Your experience has been a most entertaining one," remarked Holmes as his client paused and refreshed his memory with a huge pinch of snuff. "Pray continue your very interesting statement."

"There was nothing in the office but a couple of wooden chairs and a deal table, behind which sat a small man with a head that was even redder than mine. He said a few words to each candidate as he came up, and then he always managed to find some fault in them which would disqualify them. Getting a vacancy did not seem to be such a very easy matter, after all. However, when our turn came the little man was much more favorable to me than to any of the others, and he closed the door as we entered, so that he might have a private word with us.

"'This is Mr. Jabez Wilson,' said my assistant, 'and he is willing to fill a vacancy in the League.'

"'And he is admirably suited for it,' the other answered. 'He has every requirement. I cannot recall when I have seen anything so fine.' He took a step backward, cocked his head on one side, and gazed at my hair until I felt quite bashful. Then suddenly he plunged forward, wrung my hand, and congratulated me warmly on my success.

"'It would be injustice to hesitate,' said he. 'You will, however, I am sure, excuse me for taking an obvious precaution.' With that he seized my hair in both his hands, and tugged until I yelled with the pain. 'There is water in your eyes,' said he as he released me. 'I perceive that all is as it should be. But we have to be careful, for we have twice been deceived by wigs and once by paint. I could tell you tales of cobbler's wax which would disgust you with human nature.' He stepped over to the window and shouted through it at the top of his voice that the vacancy was filled. A groan of disappointment came up from below, and the folk all trooped away in different directions until there was not a red-head to be seen except my own and that of the manager.

"'My name,' said he, 'is Mr. Duncan Ross, and I am myself one of the pensioners upon the fund left by our noble benefactor. Are you a married man, Mr. Wilson? Have you a family?'

"I answered that I had not.

"His face fell immediately.

"'Dear me!' he said gravely, 'that is very serious indeed! I am sorry to hear you say that. The fund was, of course, for the propagation and spread of the red-heads as well as for their maintenance. It is exceedingly unfortunate that you should be a bachelor.'

"My face lengthened at this, Mr. Holmes, for I thought that I was not to have the vacancy after all; but after thinking it over for a few minutes he said that it would be all right.

"'In the case of another,' said he, 'the objection might be fatal, but we must stretch a point in favor of a man with such a head of hair as yours. When shall you be able to enter upon your new duties?'

"'Well, it is a little awkward, for I have a business already,' said I.

"'Oh, never mind about that, Mr. Wilson!' said Vincent Spaulding. 'I should be able to look after that for you.'

"'What would be the hours?' I asked.

"'Ten to two.'

"Now a pawnbroker's business is mostly done of an evening, Mr. Holmes, especially Thursday and Friday evening, which is just before pay-day; so it would suit me very well to earn a little in the mornings. Besides, I knew that my assistant was a good man, and that he would see to anything that turned up.

"'That would suit me very well,' said I. 'And the pay?'

"'Is 4 pounds a week.'

"'And the work?'

"'Is purely nominal.'

"'What do you call purely nominal?'

"'Well, you have to be in the office, or at least in the building, the whole time. If you leave, you forfeit your whole position forever. The will is very clear upon that point. You don't comply with the conditions if you budge from the office during that time.'

"'It's only four hours a day, and I should not think of leaving,' said I.

"'No excuse will avail,' said Mr. Duncan Ross; 'neither sickness nor business nor anything else. There you must stay, or you lose your billet.'

"'And the work?'

"'Is to copy out the *Encyclopaedia Britannica*. There is the first volume of it in that press. You must find your own ink, pens, and blotting-paper, but we provide this table and chair. Will you be ready to-morrow?'

"'Certainly,' I answered.

"'Then, good-bye, Mr. Jabez Wilson, and let me congratulate you once more on the important position which you have been fortunate enough to gain.' He bowed me out of the room and I went home with my assistant, hardly knowing what to say or do, I was so pleased at my own good fortune.

"Well, I thought over the matter all day, and by evening I was in low spirits again; for I had quite persuaded myself that the whole affair must be some great hoax or fraud, though what its object might be I could not imagine. It seemed altogether past belief that anyone could make such a will, or that they would pay such a sum for doing anything so simple as copying out the *Encyclopaedia Britannica*. Vincent Spaulding did what he could to cheer me up, but by bedtime I had reasoned myself out of the whole thing. However, in the morning I determined to have a look at it anyhow, so I bought a penny bottle of ink, and with a quill-pen, and seven sheets of foolscap paper, I started off for Pope's Court.

"Well, to my surprise and delight, everything was as right as possible. The table was set out ready for me, and Mr. Duncan Ross was there to see that I got fairly to work. He started me off upon the letter A, and then he left me; but he would drop in from time to time to see that all was right with me. At two o'clock he bade me good-day, complimented me upon the amount that I had written, and locked the door of the office after me.

"This went on day after day, Mr. Holmes, and on Saturday the manager came in and planked down four golden sovereigns for my week's work. It was the same next week, and the same the week after. Every morning I was there at ten, and every afternoon I left at two. By degrees Mr. Duncan Ross took to coming in only once of a morning, and then, after a time, he did not come in at all. Still, of course, I never dared to leave the room for an instant, for I was not sure when he might come, and the billet was such a good one, and suited me so well, that I would not risk the loss of it.

"Eight weeks passed away like this, and I had written about Abbots and Archery and Armour and Architecture and Attica, and hoped with diligence that I might get on to the B's before very long. It cost me something in foolscap, and I had pretty nearly filled a shelf with my writings. And then suddenly the whole business came to an end."

"To an end?"

"Yes, sir. And no later than this morning. I went to my work as usual at ten o'clock, but the door was shut and locked, with a little square of card-board hammered on to the middle of the panel with a tack. Here it is, and you can read for yourself."

He held up a piece of white card-board about the size of a sheet of note-paper. It read in this fashion:

THE RED-HEADED LEAGUE
IS
DISSOLVED.
October 9, 1890.

Sherlock Holmes and I surveyed this curt announcement and the rueful face behind it, until the comical side of the affair so completely overtopped every other consideration that we both burst out into a roar of laughter.

"I cannot see that there is anything very funny," cried our client, flushing up to the roots of his flaming head. "If you can do nothing better than laugh at me, I can go elsewhere."

"No, no," cried Holmes, shoving him back into the chair from which he had half risen. "I really wouldn't miss your case for the world. It is most refreshingly unusual. But there is, if you will excuse my saying so, something just a little funny about it. Pray what steps did you take when you found the card upon the door?"

"I was staggered, sir. I did not know what to do. Then I called at the offices round, but none of them seemed to know anything about it. Finally, I went to the landlord, who is an accountant living on the ground-floor, and I asked him if he could tell me what had become of the Red-headed League. He said that he had never heard of any such body. Then I asked him who Mr. Duncan Ross was. He answered that the name was new to him.

"'Well,' said I, 'the gentleman at No. 4.'

"'What, the red-headed man?'

"'Yes.'

"'Oh,' said he, 'his name was William Morris. He was a solicitor and was using my room as a temporary convenience until his new premises were ready. He moved out yesterday.'

"'Where could I find him?'

"'Oh, at his new offices. He did tell me the address. Yes, 17 King Edward Street, near St. Paul's.'

"I started off, Mr. Holmes, but when I got to that address it was a manufactory of artificial knee-caps, and no one in it had ever heard of either Mr. William Morris or Mr. Duncan Ross."

"And what did you do then?" asked Holmes.

"I went home to Saxe-Coburg Square, and I took the advice of my assistant. But he could not help me in any way. He could only say that if I waited I should hear by post. But that was not quite good enough, Mr. Holmes. I did not wish to lose such a place without a struggle, so, as I had heard that you were good enough to give advice to poor folk who were in need of it, I came right away to you."

"And you did very wisely," said Holmes. "Your case is an exceedingly remarkable one, and I shall be happy to look into it. From what you have told me I think that it is possible that graver issues hang from it than might at first sight appear."

"Grave enough!" said Mr. Jabez Wilson. "Why, I have lost four pound a week."

"As far as you are personally concerned," remarked Holmes, "I do not see that you have any grievance against this extraordinary league. On the contrary, you are, as I understand, richer by some 30 pounds, to say nothing of the minute knowledge which you have gained on every subject which comes under the letter A. You have lost nothing by them."

"No, sir. But I want to find out about them, and who they are, and what their object was in playing this prank—if it was a prank—upon me. It was a pretty expensive joke for them, for it cost them two and thirty pounds."

"We shall endeavor to clear up these points for you. And, first, one or two questions, Mr. Wilson. This assistant of yours who first called your attention to the advertisement—how long had he been with you?"

"About a month then."

"How did he come?"

"In answer to an advertisement."

"Was he the only applicant?"

"No, I had a dozen."

"Why did you pick him?"

"Because he was handy and would come cheap."

"At half-wages, in fact."

"Yes."

"What is he like, this Vincent Spaulding?"

"Small, stout-built, very quick in his ways, no hair on his face, though he's not short of thirty. Has a white splash of acid upon his forehead."

Holmes sat up in his chair in considerable excitement. "I thought as much," said he. "Have you ever observed that his ears are pierced for earrings?"

"Yes, sir. He told me that a gypsy had done it for him when he was a lad."

"Hum!" said Holmes, sinking back in deep thought. "He is still with you?"

"Oh, yes, sir; I have only just left him."

"And has your business been attended to in your absence?"

"Nothing to complain of, sir. There's never very much to do of a morning."

"That will do, Mr. Wilson. I shall be happy to give you an opinion upon the subject in the course of a day or two. To-day is Saturday, and I hope that by Monday we may come to a conclusion."

"Well, Watson," said Holmes when our visitor had left us, "what do you make of it all?"

"I make nothing of it," I answered frankly. "It is a most mysterious business."

"As a rule," said Holmes, "the more bizarre a thing is the less mysterious it proves to be. It is your commonplace, featureless crimes which are really puzzling, just as a commonplace face is the most difficult to identify. But I must be prompt over this matter."

"What are you going to do, then?" I asked.

"To smoke," he answered. "It is quite a three pipe problem, and I beg that you won't speak to me for fifty minutes." He curled himself up in his chair, with his thin knees drawn up to his hawk-like nose, and there he sat with his eyes closed and his black clay pipe thrusting out like the bill of some strange bird. I had come to the conclusion that he had dropped asleep, and indeed was nodding myself, when he suddenly sprang out of his chair with the gesture of a man who has made up his mind and put his pipe down upon the mantelpiece.

"Sarasate plays at the St. James's Hall this afternoon," he remarked. "What do you think, Watson? Could your patients spare you for a few hours?"

"I have nothing to do to-day. My practice is never very absorbing."

"Then put on your hat and come. I am going through the City first, and we can have some lunch on the way. I observe that there is a good deal of German music on the programme, which is rather more to my taste than Italian or French. It is introspective, and I want to introspect. Come along!"

We travelled by the Underground as far as Aldersgate; and a short walk took us to Saxe-Coburg Square, the scene of the singular story which we had listened to in the morning. It was a poky, little, shabby-genteel place, where four lines of dingy two-storied brick houses looked out into a small railed-in enclosure, where a lawn of weedy grass and a few clumps of faded laurel-bushes made a hard fight against a smoke-laden and uncongenial atmosphere. Three gilt balls and a brown board with "JABEZ WILSON" in white letters, upon a corner house, announced the place where our red-headed client carried on his business. Sherlock Holmes stopped in front of it with his head on one side and looked it all over, with his eyes shining brightly between puckered lids. Then he walked slowly up the street, and then down again to the corner, still looking keenly at the houses. Finally he returned to the pawnbroker's, and, having thumped vigorously upon the pavement with his stick two or three times, he went up to the door and knocked. It was instantly opened by a bright-looking, clean-shaven young fellow, who asked him to step in.

"Thank you," said Holmes, "I only wished to ask you how you would go from here to the Strand."

"Third right, fourth left," answered the assistant promptly, closing the door.

"Smart fellow, that," observed Holmes as we walked away. "He is, in my judgment. the fourth smartest man in London, and for daring I am not sure that he has not a claim to be third. I have known something of him before."

"Evidently," said I, "Mr. Wilson's assistant counts for a good deal in this mystery of the Red-headed League. I am sure that you inquired your way merely in order that you might see him."

"Not him."

"What then?"

"The knees of his trousers."

"And what did you see?"

"What I expected to see."

"Why did you beat the pavement?"

"My dear doctor, this is a time for observation, not for talk. We are spies in an enemy's country. We know something of Saxe-Coburg Square. Let us now explore the parts which lie behind it."

The road in which we found ourselves as we turned round the corner from the retired Saxe-Coburg Square presented as great a contrast to it as the front of a picture does to the back. It was one of the main arteries which conveyed the traffic of the City to the north and west. The roadway was blocked with the immense stream of commerce flowing in a double tide inward and outward, while the footpaths were black with the hurrying swarm of pedestrians. It was difficult to realize as we looked at the line of fine shops and stately business premises that they really abutted on the other side upon the faded and stagnant square which we had just quitted.

"Let me see," said Holmes, standing at the corner and glancing along the line, "I should like just to remember the order of the houses here. It is a hobby of mine to have an exact knowledge of London. There is Mortimer's, the tobacconist, the little newspaper shop, the Coburg branch of the City and Suburban Bank, the Vegetarian Restaurant, and McFarlane's carriage-building depot. That carries us right on to the other block. And now, Doctor, we've done our work, so it's time we had some play. A sandwich and a cup of coffee, and then off to violin-land, where all is sweetness and delicacy and harmony, and there are no red-headed clients to vex us with their conundrums."

My friend was an enthusiastic musician, being himself not only a very capable performer but a composer of no ordinary merit. All the afternoon he sat in the stalls wrapped in the most perfect happiness, gently waving his long, thin fingers in time to the music, while his gently smiling face and his languid, dreamy eyes were as unlike those of Holmes, the sleuth-hound, Holmes the relentless, keen-witted, ready-handed criminal agent, as it was possible to conceive. In his singular character the dual nature alternately asserted itself, and his extreme exactness and astuteness represented, as I have often thought, the reaction against the poetic and contemplative mood which occasionally predominated in him. The swing of his nature took him from extreme languor to devouring energy; and, as I knew well, he was never so truly formidable as when, for days on end, he had been lounging in his armchair amid his improvisations and his black-letter editions. Then it was that the lust of the chase would suddenly come upon him, and that his brilliant reasoning power would rise to the level of intuition, until those who were unacquainted with his methods would look askance at him as on a man whose knowledge was not that of other mortals. When I saw him that afternoon so enwrapped in the music at St. James's Hall I felt that an evil time might be coming upon those whom he had set himself to hunt down.

"You want to go home, no doubt, Doctor," he remarked as we emerged.

"Yes, it would be as well."

"And I have some business to do which will take some hours. This business at Coburg Square is serious."

"Why serious?"

"A considerable crime is in contemplation. I have every reason to believe that we shall be in time to stop it. But to-day being Saturday rather complicates matters. I shall want your help to-night."

"At what time?"

"Ten will be early enough."

"I shall be at Baker Street at ten."

"Very well. And, I say, Doctor, there may be some little danger, so kindly put your army revolver in your pocket." He waved his hand, turned on his heel, and disappeared in an instant among the crowd.

I trust that I am not more dense than my neighbors, but I was always oppressed with a sense of my own stupidity in my dealings with Sherlock Holmes. Here I had heard what he had heard, I had seen what he had seen, and yet from his words it was evident that he saw clearly not only what had happened but what was about to happen, while to me the whole business was still confused and grotesque. As I drove home to my house in Kensington I thought over it all, from the extraordinary story of the red-headed copier of the Encyclopaedia down to the visit to Saxe-Coburg Square, and the ominous words with which he had parted from me. What was this nocturnal expedition, and why should I go armed? Where were we going, and what were we to do? I had the hint from Holmes that this smooth-faced pawnbroker's assistant was a formidable man—a man who might play a deep game. I tried to puzzle it out, but gave it up in despair and set the matter aside until night should bring an explanation.

It was a quarter-past nine when I started from home and made my way across the Park, and so through Oxford Street to Baker Street. Two hansoms were standing at the door, and as I entered the passage I heard the sound of voices from above. On entering his room I found Holmes in animated conversation with two men, one of whom I recognized as Peter Jones, the official police agent, while the other was a long, thin, sad-faced man, with a very shiny hat and oppressively respectable frock-coat.

"Ha! Our party is complete," said Holmes, buttoning up his peajacket and taking his heavy hunting crop from the rack. "Watson, I think you know Mr. Jones, of Scotland Yard? Let me introduce you to Mr. Merryweather, who is to be our companion in to-night's adventure."

"We're hunting in couples again, Doctor, you see," said Jones in his consequential way. "Our friend here is a wonderful man for starting a chase. All he wants is an old dog to help him to do the running down."

"I hope a wild goose may not prove to be the end of our chase," observed Mr. Merryweather gloomily.

"You may place considerable confidence in Mr. Holmes, sir," said the police agent loftily. "He has his own little methods, which are, if he won't mind my saying so, just a little too theoretical and fantastic, but he has the makings of a detective in him. It is not too much to say that once or twice, as in that business of the Sholto murder and the Agra treasure, he has been more nearly correct than the official force."

"Oh, if you say so, Mr. Jones, it is all right," said the stranger with deference. "Still, I confess that I miss my rubber. It is the first Saturday night for seven-and-twenty years that I have not had my rubber."

"I think you will find," said Sherlock Holmes, "that you will play for a higher stake to-night than you have ever done yet, and that the play will be more exciting. For you, Mr. Merryweather, the stake will be some 30,000 pounds; and for you, Jones, it will be the man upon whom you wish to lay your hands."

"John Clay, the murderer, thief, smasher, and forger. He's a young man, Mr. Merryweather, but he is at the head of his profession, and I would rather have my bracelets on him than on any criminal in London. He's a remarkable man, is young John Clay. His grandfather was a royal duke, and he himself has been to Eton and Oxford. His brain is as cunning as his fingers, and though we meet signs of him at every turn, we never know where to find the man himself. He'll crack a crib in Scotland one week, and be raising money to build an orphanage in Cornwall the next. I've been on his track for years and have never set eyes on him yet."

"I hope that I may have the pleasure of introducing you to-night. I've had one or two little turns also with Mr. John Clay, and I agree with you that he is at the head of his profession. It is past ten, however, and quite time that we started. If you two will take the first hansom, Watson and I will follow in the second."

Sherlock Holmes was not very communicative during the long drive and lay back in the cab humming the tunes which he had heard in the afternoon. We rattled through an endless labyrinth of gas-lit streets until we emerged into Farrington Street.

"We are close there now," my friend remarked. "This fellow Merryweather is a bank director, and personally interested in the matter. I thought it as well to have Jones with us also. He is not a bad fellow, though an absolute imbecile in his profession. He has one positive virtue. He is as brave as a bulldog and as tenacious as a lobster if he gets his claws upon anyone. Here we are, and they are waiting for us."

We had reached the same crowded thoroughfare in which we had found ourselves in the morning. Our cabs were dismissed, and, following the guidance of Mr. Merryweather, we passed down a narrow passage and through a side door, which he opened for us. Within there was a small corridor, which ended in a very massive iron gate. This also was opened, and led down a flight of winding stone steps, which terminated at another formidable gate. Mr. Merryweather stopped to light a lantern, and then conducted us down a dark, earth-smelling passage, and so, after opening a third door, into a huge vault or cellar, which was piled all round with crates and massive boxes.

"You are not very vulnerable from above," Holmes remarked as he held up the lantern and gazed about him.

"Nor from below," said Mr. Merryweather, striking his stick upon the flags which lined the floor. "Why, dear me, it sounds quite hollow!" he remarked, looking up in surprise.

"I must really ask you to be a little more quiet!" said Holmes severely. "You have already imperilled the whole success of our expedition. Might I beg that you would have the goodness to sit down upon one of those boxes, and not to interfere?"

The solemn Mr. Merryweather perched himself upon a crate, with a very injured expression upon his face, while Holmes fell upon his knees upon the floor and, with the lantern and a magnifying lens, began to examine minutely the cracks between the stones. A few seconds sufficed to satisfy him, for he sprang to his feet again and put his glass in his pocket.

"We have at least an hour before us," he remarked, "for they can hardly take any steps until the good pawnbroker is safely in bed. Then they will not lose a minute, for the sooner they do their work the longer time they will have for their escape. We are at present, Doctor—as no doubt you have divined—in the cellar of the City branch of one of the principal London banks. Mr. Merryweather is the chairman of directors, and he will explain to you that there are reasons why the more daring criminals of London should take a considerable interest in this cellar at present."

"It is our French gold," whispered the director. "We have had several warnings that an attempt might be made upon it."

"Your French gold?"

"Yes. We had occasion some months ago to strengthen our resources and borrowed for that purpose 30,000 napoleons from the Bank of France. It has become known that we have never had occasion to unpack the money, and that it is still lying in our cellar. The crate upon which I sit contains 2,000 napoleons packed between layers of lead foil. Our reserve of bullion is much larger at present than is usually kept in a single branch office, and the directors have had misgivings upon the subject."

"Which were very well justified," observed Holmes. "And now it is time that we arranged our little plans. I expect that within an hour matters will come to a head. In the meantime Mr. Merryweather, we must put the screen over that dark lantern."

"And sit in the dark?"

"I am afraid so. I had brought a pack of cards in my pocket, and I thought that, as we were a partie carree, you might have your rubber after all. But I see that the enemy's preparations have gone so far that we cannot risk the presence of a light. And, first of all, we must choose our positions. These are daring men, and though we shall take them at a disadvantage, they may do us some harm unless we are careful. I shall stand behind this crate, and do you conceal yourselves behind those. Then, when I flash a light upon them, close in swiftly. If they fire, Watson, have no compunction about shooting them down."

I placed my revolver, cocked, upon the top of the wooden case behind which I crouched. Holmes shot the slide across the front of his lantern and left us in pitch darkness—such an absolute darkness as I have never before experienced. The smell of hot metal remained to assure us that the light was still there, ready to flash out at a moment's notice. To me, with my nerves worked up to a pitch of expectancy, there was something depressing and subduing in the sudden gloom, and in the cold dank air of the vault.

"They have but one retreat," whispered Holmes. "That is back through the house into Saxe-Coburg Square. I hope that you have done what I asked you, Jones?"

"I have an inspector and two officers waiting at the front door."

"Then we have stopped all the holes. And now we must be silent and wait."

What a time it seemed! From comparing notes afterwards it was but an hour and a quarter, yet it appeared to me that the night must have almost gone. and the dawn be breaking above us. My limbs were weary and stiff, for I feared to change my position; yet my nerves were worked up to the highest pitch of tension, and my hearing was so acute that I could not only hear the gentle breathing of my companions, but I could distinguish the deeper, heavier in-breath of the bulky Jones from the thin, sighing note of the bank director. From my position I could look over the case in the direction of the floor. Suddenly my eyes caught the glint of a light.

At first it was but a lurid spark upon the stone pavement. Then it lengthened out until it became a yellow line, and then, without any warning or sound, a gash seemed to open and a hand appeared; a white, almost womanly hand, which felt about in the centre of the little area of light. For a minute or more the hand, with its writhing fingers, protruded out of the floor. Then it was withdrawn as suddenly as it appeared, and all was dark again save the single lurid spark which marked a chink between the stones.

Its disappearance, however, was but momentary. With a rending, tearing sound, one of the broad, white stones turned over upon its side and left a square, gaping hole, through which streamed the light of a lantern. Over the edge there peeped a clean-cut, boyish face, which looked keenly about it, and then, with a hand on either side of the aperture, drew itself shoulder-high and waist-high, until one knee rested upon the edge. In another instant he stood at the side of the hole and was hauling after him a companion, lithe and small like himself, with a pale face and a shock of very red hair.

"It's all clear," he whispered. "Have you the chisel and the bags? Great Scott! Jump, Archie, jump, and I'll swing for it!"

Sherlock Holmes had sprung out and seized the intruder by the collar. The other dived down the hole, and I heard the sound of rending cloth as Jones clutched at his skirts. The light flashed upon the barrel of a revolver, but Holmes's hunting crop came down on the man's wrist, and the pistol clinked upon the stone floor.

"It's no use, John Clay," said Holmes blandly. "You have no chance at all."

"So I see," the other answered with the utmost coolness. "I fancy that my pal is all right, though I see you have got his coat-tails."

"There are three men waiting for him at the door," said Holmes.

"Oh, indeed! You seem to have done the thing very completely. I must compliment you."

"And I you," Holmes answered. "Your red-headed idea was very new and effective."

"You'll see your pal again presently," said Jones. "He's quicker at climbing down holes than I am. Just hold out while I fix the derbies."

"I beg that you will not touch me with your filthy hands," remarked our prisoner as the handcuffs clattered upon his wrists. "You may not be aware that I have royal blood in my veins. Have the goodness, also, when you address me always to say 'sir' and 'please.'"

"All right," said Jones with a stare and a snigger. "Well, would you please, sir, march upstairs, where we can get a cab to carry your Highness to the police-station?"

"That is better," said John Clay serenely. He made a sweeping bow to the three of us and walked quietly off in the custody of the detective.

"Really, Mr. Holmes," said Mr. Merryweather as we followed them from the cellar, "I do not know how the bank can thank you or repay you. There is no doubt that you have detected and defeated in the most complete manner one of the most determined attempts at bank robbery that have ever come within my experience."

"I have had one or two little scores of my own to settle with Mr. John Clay," said Holmes. "I have been at some small expense over this matter, which I shall expect the bank to refund, but beyond that I am amply repaid by having had an experience which is in many ways unique, and by hearing the very remarkable narrative of the Red-headed League."

"You see, Watson," he explained in the early hours of the morning as we sat over a glass of whisky and soda in Baker Street, "it was perfectly obvious from the first that the only possible object of this rather fantastic business of the advertisement of the League, and the copying of the Encyclopaedia, must be to get this not over-bright pawnbroker out of the way for a number of hours every day. It was a curious way of managing it, but, really, it would be difficult to suggest a better. The method was no doubt suggested to Clay's ingenious mind by the color of his accomplice's hair. The 4 pounds a week was a lure which must draw him, and what was it to them, who were playing for thousands? They put in the advertisement, one rogue has the temporary office, the other rogue incites the man to apply for it. and together they manage to secure his absence every morning in the week. From the time that I heard of the assistant having come for half wages, it was obvious to me that he had some strong motive for securing the situation."

"But how could you guess what the motive was?"

"Had there been women in the house, I should have suspected a mere vulgar intrigue. That, however, was out of the question. The man's business was a small one, and there was nothing in his house which could account for such elaborate preparations, and such an expenditure as they were at. It must, then, be something out of the house. What could it be? I thought of the assistant's fondness for photography, and his trick of vanishing into the cellar. The cellar! There was the end of this tangled clew. Then I made inquiries as to this mysterious assistant and found that I had to deal with one of the coolest and most daring criminals in London. He was doing something in the cellar—something which took many hours a day for months on end. What could it be, once more? I could think of nothing save that he was running a tunnel to some other building.

"So far I had got when we went to visit the scene of action. I surprised you by beating upon the pavement with my stick. I was ascertaining whether the cellar stretched out in front or behind. It was not in front. Then I rang the bell, and, as I hoped, the assistant answered it. We have had some skirmishes, but we had never set eyes upon each other before. I hardly looked at his face. His knees were what I wished to see. You must yourself have remarked how worn, wrinkled, and stained they were. They spoke of those hours of burrowing. The only remaining point was what they were bur-rowing for. I walked round the corner, saw the City and Suburban Bank abutted on our friend's premises, and felt that I had solved my problem. When you drove home after the concert I called upon Scotland Yard and upon the chairman of the bank directors, with the result that you have seen."

"And how could you tell that they would make their attempt to-night?" I asked.

"Well, when they closed their League offices that was a sign that they cared no longer about Mr. Jabez Wilson's presence—in other words, that they had completed their tunnel. But it was essential that they should use it soon, as it might be discovered, or the bullion might be removed. Saturday would suit them better than any other day, as it would give them two days for their escape. For all these reasons I expected them to come to-night."

"You reasoned it out beautifully," I exclaimed in unfeigned admiration "It is so long a chain, and yet every link rings true."

"It saved me from ennui," he answered, yawning. "Alas! I already feel it closing in upon me. My life is spent in one long effort to escape from the commonplaces of existence. These little problems help me to do so." "And you are a benefactor of the race," said I.

He shrugged his shoulders. "Well, perhaps, after all, it is of some little use," he remarked. "'*L'homme c'est rien—l'oeuvre c'est tout,*' as Gustave Flaubert wrote to George Sand."